SWEPT AWAY

White Dove Romances

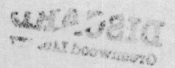

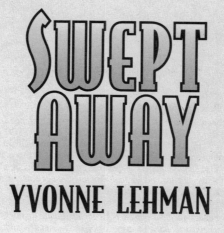

SWEPT AWAY

YVONNE LEHMAN

BETHANY HOUSE PUBLISHERS
MINNEAPOLIS, MINNESOTA 55438

Published by Bethany House Publishers
A Ministry of Bethany Fellowship, Inc.
11300 Hampshire Avenue South
Minneapolis, Minnesota 55238
Printed in the United States of America.

Library of Congress Cataloging-in-Publication Data
Lehman, Yvonne.
    Swept away / by Yvonne Lehman.
    p.   cm. — (White dove romance ; 6)
    Summary: With God on her side, Natalie remains calm
when an escaped prisoner abducts her and they both become
trapped in raging floodwaters.
    ISBN 1–55661–710–0 (pbk.)
    [1. Kidnapping—Fiction. 2. Floods—Fiction.
3. Christian life—Fiction.] I. Title. II. Series: Lehman,
Yvonne. White dove romance ; 6.
PZ7.L5322Sw   1997
[Fic]—dc21   97–33883
                                                       CIP
                                                        AC

To a very special young lady
named Bethany.

This is what the Lord says:
"Blessed is the man who trusts in the Lord,
whose confidence is in him.
He will be like a tree planted by the water
that sends out its roots by the stream."

Jeremiah 17:5a, 7–8a

One

"Slow down, Natalie!" Jill Ainsworth warned her daughter as she peered through the torrential rain hitting the windshield. "These wet roads could be treacherous."

"Sorry, Mom." Natalie eased up on the accelerator. "I just didn't want you to be late to class."

"Better late than off in a ditch somewhere. Especially in this downpour." Her mother patted Natalie's leg. "And please be careful getting to Cissy's place after you drop me off. I wouldn't have agreed to this if I'd known the weather was going to be this bad."

Seventeen-year-old Natalie Ainsworth had gotten a phone call from Cissy Stiles around five o'clock. Cissy had "the greatest news" and just *had* to tell Natalie face-to-face.

"You know I can hardly wait to hear what Cissy has to say, Mom," Natalie said. They were getting close now to Logan Junior College, where Natalie was going to drop her mother off at her night class, then drive on to Cissy's house to hear the news.

Jill laughed. "With Cissy, it's gotta be something big!"

"Right," Natalie agreed. Whatever it was, it had *better* be good to make her drive all the way to Garden Acres in this storm!

Natalie smiled to herself as she thought about her

friend Cissy, who was a year older than Natalie and a freshman in college. She was one of those people who just seemed to have everything going for her. She was beautiful for one—tall, blue eyed, and blond—and had modeled at a local department store for years. And on top of that her family had plenty of money. They lived in the most exclusive area of Garden City, in southern Illinois, where they'd all grown up together. Cissy had gotten starring roles in many school plays and community theater. Then last winter she'd been a finalist in the Top Ten agency's Dream Teen Model Search in New York City, and Natalie had been invited to go along.

"What could be bigger than being in the Top Ten competition?" Natalie wondered aloud.

"I can't imagine," Jill said, smiling brightly. "Maybe she's engaged."

Natalie gasped. "To Antonio? But . . . he's in New York."

"Well," Jill hedged, "these days, he could've just *faxed* Cissy a ring."

"Be serious, Mom," Natalie laughed. "He'd be much more romantic than that." After all, Antonio Carlo wasn't just a kid. He was out of college and working for his parents, who owned the Top Ten Modeling Agency.

"I should hope so—" Jill replied.

Her comment was cut short when the car suddenly slid on a torrent of water crossing the highway. Jill gasped as they swerved toward the center line. Headlights from approaching traffic loomed closer, and both mother and daughter held their breath as Natalie struggled to stay calm and get the car back under control.

Natalie remembered her father's words to her last winter when he had taught her how to drive on icy roads. *"Stay calm,"* he'd said. *"Don't panic, don't brake, don't jerk the steering wheel. Just go with the swerve, then gently turn the wheel and gain control.*" His words now seemed parroted by her mom, and Natalie was able to get the car back in the lane and regain control on the slick surface of the highway. She could hear her mother let out her breath as she cautioned, "Be careful, hon."

Natalie *was* a careful driver, but being reminded that water could be as treacherous as ice and that an accident could happen within seconds, she slowed further. As she carefully scanned the road ahead, she didn't say anything. She just wanted to get there now—to drop off her mom at the college, then make it to Cissy's place safely. Losing control like that really shook her up. She didn't want any more of *that* kind of excitement this evening.

Jill was quiet now, too, and as the rain grew even heavier and the visibility worsened, she also seemed to be concentrating on the road, keeping an eye out for the entrance to the college.

Hearing from Cissy had made Natalie feel closer to her boyfriend, Scott Lambert, who was in New York on a modeling shoot. He and Cissy were cousins, and although Cissy hadn't gotten a modeling contract while in New York, without even trying, Scott had! And Natalie missed him terribly.

"It's strange," Natalie said, breaking the silence, "that Cissy and I became friends."

Jill smiled lovingly at her daughter. "The Lord knew that Cissy needed a lot more than what her family's money and her own good looks could bring her." She patted her daughter's jean-clad leg again, adding proudly, "That's where you came in."

Natalie smiled. "She's a really strong Christian now. It's amazing what God can do, isn't it?"

"It sure is, honey," Jill said. "We have so much to be thankful for. There," Jill pointed through the windshield. "There's the college just ahead. You can turn in the first driveway and let me off at the side entrance."

Near the entrance leading to the Logan Junior College classrooms, a young man, his heavy clothing drenched from the downpour, huddled behind a row of boxwood hedges. Furtively, he watched the crowds of students heading for the doors, running to get out of the rain and make it to their six o'clock classes on time. He studied the parking lot and the long driveway, watching for cars and wishing, for just a moment, that he was somewhere else. "Oh, God, what am I doing?" he whispered through clenched teeth. It was the closest thing to a real prayer Henry Miller had uttered in a very long time. He lifted his face toward the darkening sky, as if God could somehow help him out of his predicament, but the blustery wind blinded his eyes and the cold rain stung his cheeks. He lowered his head. Who was he kidding? He couldn't expect God to have any part in this. After everything he'd done? *Face it, Miller, you're on your own now.*

The narrow overhang offered no protection against the biting March wind that pushed him back against the brick building, chilling him to the bone. Pulling the hood of his soggy parka closer around his face, he wiped the rain from the week-old stubble on his chin and shivered, not so much from his rain-soaked clothing, but from the knowledge that if he were caught, he'd be locked up for a long time—if the cops didn't just shoot him instead.

But his mind was made up. This might be his only chance, and he wasn't about to back out now.

His heart raced each time a car turned into the parking lot, and he shrank back as far as he could into the corner shadows, away from the glow of the light over the door. But nobody seemed to notice him. They were busy with their umbrellas or ducking their heads and running through puddles to get to the entrance.

Twice now he'd rushed out into the parking lot to

see if anyone had left a door unlocked—and hopefully the keys in the ignition. So far, no luck. He'd hurried back to the building, pretending to be going to class.

At the far end of the parking lot, looming like some hovering monster, was the prison bus in which fifteen inmates rode to an Advanced Computer class every Thursday night. The bus was parked under a streetlight, and even through the haze of rain, he could clearly see the driver on board, reading a magazine while he waited for the inmates to return from class. The driver didn't seem to be paying too much attention to his surroundings, but Henry certainly didn't want to get near enough to be noticed. All he needed was to find a car with the door unlocked. Or else he could pick the lock on an older model with the piece of wire he'd hidden in his sock. Once he got in, he was sure he could hot-wire any car. The two prison guards had already accompanied the inmates into the building. He knew it was a miracle his absence hadn't yet been noticed. But if the instructor took attendance before tonight's midterm exam, it would all be over. He didn't have much time.

Okay, Miller. Let's try again. He started to make his way out into the parking lot a third time but saw the driver peering through the window of the bus, scanning the parking lot. Henry dashed back to his hiding place. *He's gotta know something's wrong!* This was too much for the young man's jangled nerves. There had to be a better way. The rush of students had slowed now and darkness had settled in completely. He leaned his head against the cold bricks, dragged in a gulp of air, and willed himself to calm down.

He was trying to decide what to do next when he spotted another car—surely the last one—turning off the highway and heading up the long drive toward the parking lot. It stopped at the intersection stop sign where a crossroad led to the college building. Seeing that the car had passed the parking lot entrance and was heading his way, Henry's heart beat faster. He held his breath and pressed against the bushes as the car lights momentarily blinded him.

The car was making a turn. Apparently, a driver was going to let out a passenger. *Here's your chance, Miller. You'd be a fool to pass this up. It's now or never.* With his heart pounding, Henry stepped between the hedge and the building, then began making his way down behind the bushes, trying not to think about who the driver might be. But troubling thoughts crowded his mind. *So you're going to add kidnapping to your list of accomplishments, huh? What a loser!* No, he wouldn't listen. Not this time. He mustn't let anything stop him now. Pushing aside all rational thought, he rushed for the car. His hand trembled violently as he reached inside his outer pocket and clutched his weapon.

Natalie pulled up to the curb by the side entrance to the college and stopped the car. "Good luck with your test, Mom," she said as Jill grasped her book bag and reached for the door handle.

"Thanks. I'll see you at nine. Please be careful." Pulling up the hood of her rain jacket, Jill stepped out onto the curb, slammed the door shut, and hurried toward the building.

Natalie shivered as she watched her mother dash for the door. All that rain and the flashes of lightning—not to mention their frightening near miss on the road—had made her quite jumpy. A movement in the high hedges on the other side of the sidewalk startled her, and she glanced over that way. It was just the wind, she realized, blowing the hedges and throwing eerie shadows across the wet pavement. Laughing to herself, she slowly let out her breath. *Calm down, Natalie. It's just a little rainstorm.* From habit of being carefully trained by her parents, Natalie leaned over to lock the door on the passenger side. Just as she reached, she saw a blur—a huge shadow. This time she knew it wasn't just the hedge being blown by the wind. Before she could touch the lock, the door flew open and a man jumped into the car, showering Natalie with rainwater and shoving her hard against the driver's door. He clamped a hand over her mouth and pushed something hard into her side. She could feel the steamy warmth of his breath as he shouted in her face. "Drive!" he ordered.

Lord, help me! He's got a gun! Natalie had never before experienced such sudden terror. She couldn't move. She couldn't even make a sound.

"I said drive!" he growled. "And don't you even think about screaming, you hear?" Slowly, he took his hand off her mouth, but the weapon remained in place, painfully pushing against her ribs. "Nice and easy, now . . . just do as I say and you won't get hurt. We're gonna drive out of here like nothing's the matter. You got that?"

She glanced toward the entrance in hopes that her mother would see her still sitting there at the curb and wonder what was wrong. But no one was there. All she could see through the double glass doors was an empty hallway. *Everyone's in class.* Panic seized her so badly she thought she might faint.

She found her voice enough to blurt out, "If it's the car you want, why don't you just take it and let me off here? I won't tell anyone, I promise." Natalie knew that was a bluff, but she had to try.

"Yeah right . . . and have every cop in the county on top of me in five minutes. Now move! Before I have to use this thing."

Natalie swallowed hard and nodded at the man, then slowly reached for the controls with trembling hands and feet. As they pulled away from the curb, her mind was racing. *What can I do, Lord? What can I do?*

I mustn't go with him! This was worse than her worst nightmare. *This can't be happening . . . it just can't!* Her father's words, *"Don't panic, don't swerve, don't brake,"* didn't apply now. And she seemed to have drawn in her breath but was unable to let it out. She had no instructions, except the voice of the intruder.

"Don't try anything funny," he warned.

Oh, nothing about this is funny! Natalie couldn't even ease her hand over to the door handle. It was glued to the steering wheel. She wanted to yell for help, but her throat had closed. There was no one around to hear, anyway. *Oh, God, help me!* was the desperate prayer pulsing through her mind and body.

Somewhere in the depths of her consciousness, Natalie remembered having discussions with her friends about being in just such a situation. What would they do? Someone had suggested they'd wreck the car, drive it into a building. But she was already past the college building. There was nothing but road and parking lots ahead, and then the highway.

"Keep both hands where I can see them," he ordered. "Do anything tricky and you're dead. And I'll go back and get the woman you let out at the door."

Natalie's heart seemed to be lurching out of her chest. She couldn't speak. He wouldn't really go back for her mom—would he? Was he just trying to scare her into doing what he said? Reluctantly, she stepped down harder on the gas pedal, and the car eased toward the main road.

"Turn right onto the highway," he said.

Natalie braked at the intersection and watched the traffic, which was moving more slowly than usual and spraying water all around. Maybe she could drive out in front of a car . . . try to get out in the confusion and make a run for it. But he might shoot her right there. She didn't know what he had in mind and was afraid

16

to even think of possibilities.

At the four-way stop, she had to look in all directions. Visibility was awful in the pouring rain. The windows were getting steamed up from his heavy breathing. The car was filled with the odor of damp clothing. A thought occurred that someone said you could smell fear. She thought she did. The smell made goose bumps all over her body and seemed to settle into her bones like some dread disease.

Her quick glance swept over him when she had to look toward the right. Startled, Natalie recognized the uniform. The khaki pants, the olive green parka with a hood. This was an inmate from the federal prison where her dad worked! And he was escaping. Her dad had told her that a lot of community people were fearful of escaped prisoners. But he'd said an escapee just wants to get away, doesn't really want to stick around long enough to hurt anyone—even the most hardened criminal. This gave her some measure of hope, but her dad had never explained what happens if a prisoner takes a hostage.

Then a greater fear rose in her. *What if he knows that Dad works at the prison? Maybe he knows who I am, and he's doing this out of some kind of revenge against Dad!*

"You could have turned then," the man growled.

Natalie tried to speak, but words wouldn't come. She lifted her right hand helplessly. It was trembling, like the rest of her body. "I . . . I can't," she gasped.

"Just settle down and you won't get hurt. I just want the car. But I can't let you go yet—not until we're plenty far away from any phones. I can't have you calling the cops." Then he grabbed the steering wheel, ordering, "Now step on it!"

The car careened out onto the highway. They skidded on the rain-soaked road, swerved toward the gravel shoulder, then turned back, almost crossing the center line.

"You're trying to kill us!" the man screamed.

Natalie was terrified to have him near her. She could feel his wet clothes soaking through her dry ones. She steadied the car the best she could.

Okay, Natalie. Calm down. He says he just wants the car. Maybe he's telling the truth. She could only pray he wouldn't change his mind. But even if he did let her off in the middle of nowhere, he might decide it wouldn't be safe. She'd get back to town eventually and would be able to give the police a complete description. He might decide to tie her up and leave her in some abandoned building . . . or worse. *Please, God, please don't let him kill me.* With a sinking feeling, she realized she and her mom had gone to a gas station before they left Garden City. The car had a full tank of gas. They could drive a very long way before having to stop.

They were headed out of town on Highway 13, opposite the direction she had come with her mom. Highway 13 soon became 149. Natalie's fingers tightened around the steering wheel when he spoke again.

"I'll let you out a few miles from here if you're good. If not . . ."

He didn't finish, and Natalie tried not to think anymore about this stranger's plans for her, or what he meant by saying, "If you're good . . ."

Two

"Come on over, Katlyn," Cissy invited when her next-door neighbor answered the phone. "I'm having a party!"

"Are you crazy? It's raining gorillas out there," Katlyn quipped.

Cissy only laughed. "Hey, it's liquid sunshine!" she exclaimed. "Anyway, you can leave from your garage and drive into ours. Ever thought of that?"

"Not really, Cissy. The way it's been raining, our garage might be a swimming pool by now."

"Okay, be like that. I guess you don't want to hear my great news."

Katlyn became all ears. "News? What news? Tell me what's going on."

"No way! Not unless you're here—up close and personal," Cissy insisted.

Katlyn groaned. "Okay, okay. Who's going to be there?"

"Oh, just a few of my best friends—the ones brave enough to venture out in this downpour."

She heard Katlyn hesitate before asking, "Natalie too?"

Cissy sighed. Katlyn was much kinder to Natalie these days since she'd had her own experience with God. But Katlyn still wanted Scott Lambert for herself, and that made it hard for her to completely accept Natalie. "She's my friend, Katlyn."

"But she's so . . . ordinary."

Although Natalie's family wasn't wealthy and she wasn't drop-dead gorgeous, she was far from ordinary. Natalie's faith in God seemed to touch everyone she came in contact with, and when anyone got to know her, they just couldn't help liking her. Scott had become close to Natalie because she'd helped him through his personal family troubles when his mother was having problems with an alcohol addiction.

"I know how you feel, Katlyn"—Cissy tried to be understanding—"but I think you'd feel differently if you got to know Natalie better. She helped Scott through a really tough time, and it's only natural that they've become close."

Cissy could almost feel the negative vibes coming through the phone as Katlyn complained, "I know, but Scott's a model now. He could have any girl he wants."

Cissy didn't say the obvious—that *Natalie* was the girl he wanted. One of these days a guy would come into Katlyn's life, and she'd forget about Scott. In the meantime, Cissy would try to keep the peace and be a good friend to both Katlyn and Natalie.

"Well, like it or not, I invited Natalie," Cissy said without apology. She glanced at the hands of the small golden clock on a shelf in the living room and saw that it was almost six-thirty. "She should have been here by now. She was going to drop her mom off at Logan Junior College, then come by."

"I can't imagine her parents letting her out on a night like this," Katlyn said. "You know how strict they are." Her voice was sounding more and more like the old Katlyn, before she'd given her life to the Lord. "Except when it comes to letting her go off to New York with Scott."

"C'mon, Katlyn." Cissy was getting angry now. "You know they weren't alone. Scott's mom was there. My mom was there. I was there—"

Katlyn laughed. "You? Some chaperone! You were modeling and getting your own new guy—a gorgeous one at that!"

This time Cissy agreed with Katlyn. Antonio had come home with Scott over the holidays, and they'd been able to spend more time together. That had been super. She had to admit that she herself would be green with envy if Antonio took off with another girl. *Trying to live the way Jesus wants us to isn't always easy*, she reminded herself. Both she and Katlyn had a lot of growing to do. "I've gotta make some more calls, Katlyn. Come on over if you want to . . . if you want to hear the news, that is."

"Let me guess. I'll bet one of the winning models had to drop out and you're going to be the replacement. Right? That's your great news!"

Cissy laughed. "I'm only telling in person."

"Frankly, I wouldn't miss it. Be over in a flash."

Cissy hung up and thought about who she should call next but found herself concerned about Natalie, who really should have been here by now. Cissy's home in Garden Acres was not that far from Logan Junior College. She thought Natalie had said her mom's class was at six, but maybe she'd said seven. Cissy told herself to stop worrying. Katlyn was right about one thing. Most likely Mrs. Ainsworth decided Natalie shouldn't drive in this rough weather. And, too, if Natalie had tried to call, she might not have gotten through. Telephone lines in some areas could easily have come down in such high winds.

Dismissing her concerns about Natalie, Cissy turned her attention back to her party. *Now, let's see*, she mused. *Who to call next?*

Natalie drove along the highway for what seemed like an eternity. Every muscle in her body was tensed, and her eyes ached from trying to see something that looked familiar. She thought this road would eventually end at Highway 3. That was the road leading to Lake Oakwood, where she'd spent several days with Scott and his family last summer. Oh, how she wished Scott were with her now, instead of this . . . this stranger. But he was going to let her go. He'd said that. He just wanted the car. She'd just have to believe and pray that her dad was right about escaped prisoners wanting to get far away as quickly as they could.

It was completely dark now and there were no streetlights on the highway, making it impossible to see more than a few feet ahead. In the glow of the headlights, the slanting rain stabbed the road with long, thin silver spikes.

Why didn't I run into a car or swerve into a ditch or something? Natalie asked herself. But she hadn't. Now she could only keep praying over and over, *God, help me.*

They were miles now from Garden City. Surely he would let her out soon—if he wasn't lying. There was only an occasional car passing and none ahead or behind them.

"Okay," he said finally, "up ahead. We'll pull over."

Natalie felt a surge of relief and began to slow the car. As she pulled off onto the shoulder where he was pointing and stopped, a set of headlights glared through the windshield. In the faint glow, they could both make out the bubble-gum lights on top of the car.

"Police!" the prisoner shouted. "Keep going!"

"Just let me out first," Natalie pleaded. "Then you can take the car. They're not coming after you. . . . See? They went right past us."

"Shut up and drive!"

Natalie felt the man's gun pressing harder into her ribs, and she started to cry. *Please, God, don't let him kill me.*

"You're safer with me anyway. I'm not going to dump you on the side of the road in this weather."

Natalie couldn't believe her ears. *Safer with him? What does he mean by that?* A wave of nausea gripped her at the realization that she might be in the hands of a real psycho. What to do? Suddenly she remembered the cellular phone in the glove compartment. Maybe she could suggest he let her call for someone to come get her. But he'd never do that. It would mean the police would be on his trail just as quickly—just as they would have if he'd left her behind at the college.

At least the thought of the cell phone gave her a slim ray of hope. At some point, maybe she could get to it and dial 9–1–1.

"Now, look," he said roughly. "Neither of us is getting out of this car, and one of us is going to get this car moving. Now, what's it going to be?"

Natalie couldn't bear the thought of his climbing over her, or her climbing past him. And yet she couldn't believe he wanted her with him for "her safety." As she pulled back out onto the highway, she tried with all her might to think clearly—to find some plan. Because of the weather, Cissy would simply think she'd changed her mind when she didn't show up at her house. And her mom wouldn't even know she was missing until she got out of class at nine o'clock. Over two more hours would pass before anybody would even suspect she was missing.

What can I do?

There was no one to help her.

Natalie reminded herself that God had brought Cissy safely through a tornado. Couldn't He bring her safely through this experience? He could, yes, but . . . *would* He? Obviously, God didn't stop all the bad things in the world. He let people make their own choices—even bad ones. And as hard as it was to believe at this moment, she knew that God loved even this man beside her—loved him enough to let him make his own choices, for good or evil. She touched her white dove pin, which was fastened on her shirt beneath her jacket. As a symbol of God's Spirit, it brought some comfort—reminding her that God was always with her, that He would never leave her. A verse of Scripture leaped into her mind—"even unto the end of the world." Was this the end?

She heard the command, "Faster!" and as if she had turned into some kind of puppet, with this criminal pulling the strings, she obeyed.

Natalie obeyed again when the inmate told her to turn left onto Highway 3. She knew this highway ran along the Mississippi River. So they were heading south. Her family had come this way when they'd visited the Shawnee National Forest. Another time, they'd visited the Trail of Tears. She shivered involuntarily. She didn't want to think of anything unpleasant. *"I'll let you go if you're good,"* he'd said. Maybe . . . just maybe . . .

Then he ordered her to turn off the highway onto a barely visible side road. Every fiber of her being protested. Even the rain seemed to protest as it beat down unmercifully. But she had no choice. She turned off onto the waterlogged, secluded side road that was dark and unpaved. Tree limbs scraped the car on the narrow, bumpy road. There were no cars, no lights, no houses.

"This is a shortcut to where I'm going," the inmate said, leaning forward, as if he, too, were having trouble seeing what lay ahead. The weather was growing worse, the rain falling even harder. Every dent in the road was filled with water. Reflecting in the headlights, a hazy mist made the world seem like the twilight zone.

Natalie drove on and on, feeling as though her fingers were permanently glued to the steering wheel. Her eyes burned as she stared straight ahead, not even wanting to blink, for fear she'd run off the road and make this guy angry. They were all alone in the dismal black night. The hazy glow of the car lights revealed dark tree trunks and swaying bare branches reaching toward the car with monstrous, groping hands ready to clutch her in their gnarled fingers.

A stream of water was pouring across the road now, and she could feel the car being buffeted by the force of it against the tires. Where was he taking her? They were obviously getting closer to the river, and she began to worry that the water across the road was only going to get deeper. Up ahead a sudden flash of light startled her. *What was that? Another car?* Maybe she could run into it. Or maybe just block the road and force them to stop. But then she'd be endangering other people's lives as well. Maybe the prisoner would shoot her, then kill whoever was in the other car.

As they moved closer to the light, she could see that it wasn't moving. And it wasn't a car. She slowed to a stop. Directly ahead was a barricade across the road, its circles of light flashing a warning.

"We can't go on," Natalie said. "The road must be flooded."

"Well, we aren't going back," he growled, pulling the hood of the parka closer around his face.

Now what? Natalie wondered with a skip of her heartbeat.

Before she could think of anything to do, he reached over and grabbed the keys out of the ignition, pulled open the Velcro closing of his jacket pocket, dropped the keys in, then refastened it. To her chagrin, he opened the glove compartment and rifled through it, took the cell phone, and put that in his pocket with the keys.

Dashed! Her one last hope was completely dashed! She dared not look at him. Not even when he ordered her to move over to the passenger side. Rather than have him force her, she nodded that she would move.

Could she jump out and run after he was out of the car?

As if reading her mind, he warned, "Don't try anything stupid," and he patted his right-hand pocket. He got out and was almost blown off his feet by the wind. He steadied himself by catching hold of the door. The rain was beating down furiously. "Now move over here," he shouted to make himself heard over the raging elements.

Natalie did, then with effort he managed to slam the door shut.

Could I ever get away in this awful storm? she questioned. As she watched the man making his way to the barrièr, looking so ominously like a dark shadow one second, and lighting up in the eerie yellow glow of the headlights the next, she had her doubts. Maybe if she got out of the car undetected, she could hide in the dark behind some tree. But he was having difficulty keeping his balance in the fast-moving water, although it was only ankle-deep. And he kept looking back to ensure she was still in the car.

So she sat waiting . . . trembling. . . .

Three

Antonio! Cissy Stiles sighed as she stood for a moment, gazing at the huge crystal punch bowl on the breakfast bar separating the long family room from the open kitchen. She remembered the last party she'd thrown, when Antonio Carlo had flown in from New York with Scott. He and Scott had become friends since Scott had been signed by the Carlos' modeling agency.

Absently, she tucked a strand of her short corn-silk hair behind one ear, and her fingers grazed her cheek—feeling again Antonio's kiss as the two of them had stood on this very spot. She could see him gazing at her with those intent dark brown eyes, his curly brown hair framing his handsome Spanish features.

Talking with him on the phone today only made her miss him more.

"More punch, Cissy?"

"Huh? Oh . . ." Cissy said, returning to the present. "No thanks, Cornelia." She felt herself blush as if her housekeeper had read her mind. The sly grin on Cornelia's face indicated she had. After all, the older woman had teased her about Antonio at Christmastime. Cissy turned away from the kitchen with a flip of her wrist, a trait she'd picked up for one of the characters she'd played in local theater. "I'd better rejoin my guests."

Cornelia lifted another tray of assorted hors

d'oeuvres and served the guests as Cissy thoughtfully surveyed them. The group was small. Her circle of friends had changed some in the past two years. Most of them had gone away to well-known colleges, some abroad. Only Amanda Brooke and Cissy attended the nearby university—Amanda by choice and Cissy because of her rebellious period when she'd tried to elope instead of applying to colleges.

A smile crossed Cissy's face. Who would have thought she'd become so involved with the college class at church? Who would have thought she'd go to a local university? Who would have thought she'd still want to be close friends with seniors in high school? But here was Katlyn. And she'd invited Natalie's best friend, Ruthie Ryan, who couldn't come tonight because she was studying for a big math test tomorrow. And Natalie . . . where was Natalie?

Cissy looked at her watch. After seven o'clock. Her glance toward the patio revealed darkness and heavy, driving rain spattering the glass doors. Concern nudged at Cissy's mind, but she brushed it aside. Natalie had probably decided to wait until the rain slackened.

"Okay, you guys," she began, walking toward the center of the room, where a long couch and two love seats faced each other. Two girls from the church college class walked over and sat on a love seat. Across from them sat Katlyn and Amanda. On the long couch were four girls, one she'd met at the university, another who had decided against college and was now modeling almost full time for area stores, and two others she'd acted with in local theater. She hadn't invited any guys, feeling they wouldn't know how to appreciate this.

Although Cissy had always enjoyed being the center of attention, she realized there was a fine line between being proud of achievements and being egotistical. Since becoming a Christian, she was seeing faults in herself she'd never realized before.

"I guess no one else is coming," she began, "so I'll tell you why you're here."

Everyone quieted down and looked at Cissy, waiting for the big announcement.

"Now I feel self-conscious," Cissy laughed.

"Not Cissy Stiles!" quipped Katlyn. "Now, come on. You've kept us in suspense long enough."

"Well, if you insist," Cissy replied dramatically, which drew genuine smiles and looks of anticipation.

Cissy didn't want to sound as though she were her own greatest admirer, nor did she want to put herself down, but she felt she had to preface her announcement with a little background. "You know I was chosen as one of the Top Ten Modeling Agency finalists in the Dream Teen Model Search and went to New York over Thanksgiving break."

They nodded. That was history now!

"And you know I didn't make it to the top three, who got national recognition and tons of prizes."

"But you were a winner just being one of the ten," said Amanda.

"Right . . ." Cissy lifted an eyebrow. "So was the politician running for president who came in second. He *lost*! If you don't win first place, you're called a loser."

"Not when you land a prize like Antonio Carlo!" Katlyn said and everyone agreed.

"Well, I'm not all that upset . . . considering," Cissy laughed. "But I have to admit I *was* disappointed about the contest. I really thought it was God's will for me to go in that direction. And since then, I haven't been completely sure what God has in mind for me. But today I think He's given me an answer."

All her friends stopped eating and drinking, giving her their undivided attention.

"A publisher of a national Christian magazine was

at a gathering with the Carlos, and during the conversation, the Carlos mentioned my testimony. They showed the publisher my picture and the newspaper article about how I became a Christian, and the magazine wants to sign me on as a model!"

After all the exclamations of delight and congratulations died down, Amanda said thoughtfully, "So something *did* come from your involvement with that modeling contest."

Cissy nodded. Amanda had not made a commitment to the Lord, but of all her friends, Amanda had asked the most questions and seemed to be sincerely considering what God could mean in her life. "Yes, I think it was a test for me, Amanda," she said. "I needed a change in my attitude. I'm learning that the most important thing in life isn't your appearance, although God can use that, too, if your attitude is right. I think being a model for a Christian magazine will give me the chance to talk to younger teens about God, and I'll tell them that only when we give our lives to Him can we be truly beautiful—on the inside."

No one seemed to know what to say. Then Katlyn asked, "So what happens next?"

Cissy's smile was radiant, and her eyes shone with anticipation. "My first assignment is to be on the cover of their magazine. I'll go to New York—"she paused and grinned slyly—"and see Antonio again."

They all laughed. Cissy looked toward the kitchen, where Cornelia winked and nodded, meaning Cissy had done well in her announcement. That was a change, too. A couple of years ago, Cissy wouldn't have considered whether or not Cornelia approved of her. It was amazing how God's Spirit in a person changed one's perspective.

Cissy smiled at Cornelia as the woman came forward with another plate of goodies.

Cissy silently thanked God that she had been able

to give Him the credit for working in her life, instead of building a barricade between herself and her friends.

———⌒———

Natalie sat shivering in the car, wondering what her friends and family were doing. Did anyone even suspect yet that she was missing? She watched her abductor as he strained to shove the barricade to the side of the road. Then the drenched convict plodded back to the car through water that had now risen above his ankles and climbed into the driver's seat. He drove past the row of lights that flashed an orange-yellow warning into the black night, giving Natalie an eerie feeling of Halloween. Maybe this was a nightmare. Such a thing couldn't really be happening to her—could it?

To Natalie's surprise, he then stopped the car, got out, and replaced the barricade. Why was he doing that? To keep others from getting caught on a flooded road? Maybe he wasn't so heartless after all. On second thought, she realized, leaving the barricade at the side of the road would be like leaving a trail for the police to follow.

He turned on the radio and found the local station. The announcer was saying certain communities had been evacuated. When he said the roads to Cape Girardeau in Missouri were closed, the prisoner muttered under his breath, which made Natalie think he must have been headed there. Flood warnings and watches were out for several counties.

"We'll go the back way," he said. "I've seen it much worse. We can make it."

Natalie gripped the passenger seat with all her might and strained to see ahead. She held her breath when he eased through water that must surely be covering the tires. The water was steadily rising higher. At the barricade it had been ankle-deep. Now it was tire-deep. What next?

As if in answer, a monotonous roar reached her ears—like the sound of the ocean—then suddenly the road was covered with water. A lake had formed right in front of them! The prisoner backed up, then turned the car toward the right.

"Wh-what's happening?" Natalie asked when the headlights shone on a high rock wall and he maneuvered the car toward it, then upward into the black night. "Where are we going?"

"The levee," the prisoner answered.

"Levee?" Natalie questioned. Wasn't the levee made out of dirt and rocks? You couldn't drive on something like that . . . could you? Unless you were crazy! And what river was this, sounding like an ocean out of control? It had to be the Mississippi if they were headed for Cape Girardeau. But could it be the Ohio? Could they have gone that far south? She wanted to know, but she didn't want to ask questions and get him angry or distract him from driving. They were moving upward on a steep slant, and she could see nothing but the narrow strip of road that didn't look wide enough for even one car.

"The Mississippi is just ahead," he said.

"Oh" was all she could answer. She couldn't take her eyes from the few feet of gravel revealed by the headlights. She felt that if her glance moved to either side, so would the car. Besides, there was really nothing on either side to see—only blackness. Not even a guardrail, or a post, or anything—just . . . space.

"I've done this before," he said quietly, as if talking to himself. "It's used in times of emergency," then added, "like now."

The car crawled along this non-road with nothing but night on each side. She could hear the roar and feel the vibration of the river, in all its angry force, pushing against the levee. How long could it hold? Natalie had never been so terrified in her life. She was glad he didn't speak as he eased through the waterlogged gravel.

"We should be getting close to the other side," he said finally, and Natalie felt like giving a sigh of relief. Then he shouted, "Oh no!"

Out of the darkness rushed the foam-tipped river—heading straight for them. She watched in horror as the water crashed into the end of the levee and sloshed water onto the windshield. Water splashed over the car, and Natalie threw her arms up as if to ward it off. The prisoner slammed the car into reverse and began to back away, but Natalie felt he couldn't possibly see behind them.

Finally, she realized the water was veering down along the left side of them, making that section a raging river as angry as the great Mississippi on their right, which had now risen to the top of the levee and was licking at the gravel road. What could they possibly do? They were trapped on a narrow strip of soggy earth, totally surrounded by water!

She couldn't help the strangled sob that rose to her throat. She felt totally helpless—like during the tornado last spring. But then Scott had been with her. How very different this was!

But it had not been Scott who'd saved her life during the tornado. With that thought, she slowly moved her hand inside her jacket and felt the little white dove pin. She unfastened it, brought it out, and, after clasping it firmly in her hand as she prayed, raised her hands to fasten it on the outside of her jacket, where she could see it at a glance.

"What are you doing?" the prisoner asked suddenly, as if a movement from her might send him into a rage.

"I'm . . . fastening my white dove pin on the outside of my jacket so I can touch it and see it."

"Why?" he demanded.

Should I go into a long explanation? she wondered, just as she heard a long sigh come from him.

"You think that will help?" he asked.

She wasn't sure if his question was sincere or simply sarcastic. *Does he think this is a weapon to use against him?* she wondered. Surely he couldn't feel threatened by something so small. On second thought, there was nothing stronger than what the little white dove symbolized. *Maybe he can take my pin away,* she was thinking, *but he can't take God from me. The Bible promises that nothing can separate us from the love of God,* she reminded herself.

"It's a symbol of God's Spirit," she said quietly, brushing the tears from her cheeks. She held her breath in anticipation of what he might do.

To her surprise, he didn't say or do a thing—just remained strangely silent. Natalie wondered if she should say any more but decided to keep quiet, grateful that he didn't take the pin away from her.

The water continued to rage outside the car, but inside, Natalie could hear only her own breathing, and his, as they sat with the engine and the lights off. She felt the coldness creeping in. There was no light on the clock now to indicate the time was getting closer to when someone might come and look for her. How would anyone know where she was? But they *would* look everywhere . . . wouldn't they? She glanced toward her abductor when he made a movement, and in the shadows, she saw him pull the hood off his head.

"My name is Henry," he said. The sudden sound of his voice startled her, but his tone was subdued now, no longer frantic. "I never intended anything like this to happen. I don't want anybody to get hurt. I'm sorry about this."

The man is apologizing? Natalie thought. *Is he afraid*

we're about to die and now he wants to get right with God?

Somehow, Natalie believed he was genuinely sorry. Her greatest fear now was not of him but of the rising water, the raging Mississippi, nature going crazy. She felt sure his apology meant he thought they were going to die. His next words confirmed it.

"Do you pray?" he asked. She thought for sure his voice trembled.

Was he kidding? She hadn't stopped praying!

"Yes," she said tentatively. "You . . . want me to pray?"

He nodded. "I think you'd better. I'm not . . . too good at it."

She closed her eyes. Even that was a relief from having strained to see what was happening outside in the darkness, to glimpse some sign of life, some hope that help was on the way.

"Lord," she began, "I don't understand why you let this happen. I don't know what to pray for. But . . . we're asking for your help. And I know you see us. We're scared. We need to remember that you are with us. You can save us if you want to. That's what I want. And I think it's what Henry wants. But most important is what you want us to do with our lives. It's out of our hands . . . and in yours. If this is the end, then help us be brave and . . . take us to heaven. In Jesus' name. Amen."

Natalie sniffed and wiped her eyes. She looked toward Henry. Somehow it was easier now—now that he was not just an escaped convict but a person with a name. He turned his face away from her, and she wondered if he were crying. If he panicked, he might do something weird. After all, he had a gun.

As if he had read her mind, his arm moved and she heard the Velcro rip. Then he drew out his hand. Was he going to call for help on the cell phone? Or was he going for his gun?

Natalie drew in her breath.

Then he turned on the headlights. She looked. The rain seemed to have slackened some, but straight ahead was still a sea of water. His movement brought her attention back to him. He opened the door and seemed to be testing the ground with his left foot, then leaned farther out.

Was he going to jump? She couldn't just sit there and do nothing. Maybe she could see his face before . . .

"Henry?" she said weakly.

He turned his head to look over his shoulder at her. The reflection of the car lights turned his profile into a garish yellow color, revealing a stubbly beard just beginning to grow out. In that instant, she saw what seemed to be a glimmer of concern before he turned away again, as if he couldn't meet her eyes.

She got the impression he wasn't very old—early twenties maybe. For the first time since her abduction, she began to wonder who this young man was. What had he done? Why was he risking escape? He must truly be desperate. She thought of Zac, Scott's twenty-year-old brother, who'd thought his life was over only a few months ago. Now things had changed for him; God had helped him. Could she say that to Henry? Would it mean anything to him?

Before she could say anything, he surprised her by stepping out into the rain, holding on to the car door. What was he doing? she wondered. There couldn't be much room out there on that narrow levee.

He got back into the car, shivering, and she felt cold drops of water splash on her face and hands. The air in the car was colder, too, and she hugged her arms close to her chest.

"The water doesn't seem as high as it was," he said. "The reason for the levee is to hold back the waters of the Mississippi. And the reason for the valley on the other side is so floodwaters can run off." He reached over and switched off the lights again.

In the silence that followed, Natalie thought the wind had abated. And perhaps the rain wasn't falling as furiously. But she worried about the condition of the levee itself. Even if they stayed above the floodwaters, she thought this narrow strip of levee would become so muddy they'd just mire up in it—like being stuck in quicksand.

She looked at Henry, who sat for a moment staring straight ahead. She heard him clear his throat before drawing in a breath. "Thanks for praying," he said on an exhale. "I used to be a Christian. At least I thought I was. But my whole life has gone haywire."

His voice sounded as constricted as hers had felt since he jumped into the car, making her life a nightmare.

"Then maybe—" She stopped suddenly. What could she say? She'd been about to say that prison might have been the best thing for him if it stopped his life of crime and made him think more seriously. But maybe she shouldn't let him know she recognized the prison clothing. Besides, she didn't want him to think she was preaching at him or criticizing. Instead she simply said, "I'm very sorry, Henry." She was still wary of the man, but he didn't seem to want to harm her anymore, and she found herself beginning to feel a little compassion for him.

She heard his deep sigh. "I've got to get to Val . . . my wife. She's filing for divorce. And she's planning to kill our baby. I just hope I'm not too late to stop her."

Four

Sean Jacson sat in his dad's service station watching giant rivulets of rainwater streak down the glass front, thinking about which friends to call. He had the charts ready in his notebook. All he needed was a little privacy to make his calls and set the time and place to pick up the money.

He and his dad were eating a late supper of burgers and fries. "I don't think too many people will venture out in this downpour," Mr. Jacson said after swallowing a last bite of burger and washing it down with a gulp of soda. "Might be a good time for me to check out the brakes in your car."

"Thanks, Dad. I've got some homework I can do," Sean said, trying to sound nonchalant.

His dad smiled. "Good to see you hitting the books that way, son."

"Yep!" Sean balled up his fist and hit at the notebook he'd laid out beside the phone. *Would you hit me, Dad*, he wondered briefly, *if you knew I was a* book*ie?*

He laughed at his own joke. His dad had always been quick with the punches. That was one reason, among others, that Sean's mom had divorced him. He remembered with regret how close he had come to being just like his dad—hitting his girlfriend, Ruthie. All because he hated his dad for the way he'd treated him all his life. Of course,

Ruthie had finally broken up with him. It served him right. No girl should put up with that kind of treatment. He knew now just how wrong he'd been.

But he'd changed a lot since then—learned a few lessons. Actually, both Sean and his dad had turned over a new leaf lately. His dad was making a major effort to act decently toward Sean, and Sean himself had stopped peddling drugs—had even quit his job at the food warehouse to get away from the dealers who bought from him. He smiled to himself as he thought about his new life. Why, compared to what I used to be, I'm practically a saint! Maybe Ruthie'll take me back one of these days—when she sees how I've changed.

Mr. Jacson dumped his trash into the wastebasket and headed for the door leading to the mechanics' bay, where Sean's '67 Olds was parked.

As soon as his father was out of sight, Sean opened the notebook and looked at the chart. "Shawnee High" was written across the top and "Herrin High" down the side. The page was blocked off into squares, each representing a possible score. There were still several blank blocks on the chart. Next week was the big game. He'd get more bets tomorrow at school. He wondered briefly what Ruthie would think about a little harmless betting. He knew she didn't approve of gambling, but this was just a game. She'd probably be okay with it, he decided, but not her stick-in-the-mud best friend, Natalie Ainsworth. *That Miss Priss doesn't believe in any kind of real fun!*

After stuffing the last two fries into his mouth, Sean wiped his mouth and fingers on the napkin, jabbed it and his burger wrapper into the fries carton, and arced it toward the wastebasket, where it landed squarely in the can. "Score!" he yelled, jumping off the stool. *I'll bet I could stick it to you, Mr. Stick Gordon, basketball star. You're not so great*, he thought wryly. If only Ruthie didn't think so. He'd seen the way those two had been eyeing each other lately. And Stick his one-time friend, too. It was enough to turn his stomach.

So what if I'm not a big basketball star? There are other games to play. And I know how to make a few bucks off ol' Stick—even if he doesn't like to be bet on.

Sean grinned at the wastebasket. This way, he could win without exerting all that physical energy. Wasn't that the way *real* businessmen reached the top?

Valerie Miller was alone in the little farmhouse that had belonged to her grandparents before they died. Now it belonged to her father, and he had rented it to Val and Henry at a very low monthly payment. "So you can save for a down payment on a house of your own," he'd said.

But now, there were no savings. There would be no down payment. They'd get no house of their own.

Val had filed for divorce—had pawned her wedding rings. Maybe she could earn enough money soon to buy them back.

No! She knew better than that. She'd never get them back. What would she do with them anyway? Her marriage was over. Maybe it never had a chance from the beginning.

Val sat in the dark room on the couch, across from the woodstove, staring at the flickering flames through the glass in the door. The glass was separated by steel strips, shaped like small pieces of pie, which were almost completely blackened with soot. *Like my life*, she thought dismally. *I feel like I'm divided up into little pieces like that glass . . . stained . . . falling apart.*

She covered her ears with her hands to stop the thoughts—closed her eyes to stop the tears. She fumbled for the remote and flicked on the TV. There was nothing in particular she wanted to watch. She just needed the noise. Needed the distraction.

She'd told herself she wanted this night alone at the farmhouse to think. But there really was nothing more to think about. Her mind was made up. She'd already told Henry when she visited him last Sunday—that was the last visit. She never wanted to see him again. As cruel as that seemed, she knew it was for his own good.

Val jumped from the couch, stumbled over to the front window, and pushed aside the lace curtain. All she could see, however, was the flashing from the TV, like some kind of warning signal, against the reflection of a forlorn girl. Her hair was scraggly and her makeup washed off from having been doused by the rain when she'd come home earlier from her sales job at the department store in Cape Girardeau.

She'd changed from a dress and heels into jeans and a sweatshirt but hadn't brushed her hair. Her reflection in the window looked incredibly young, but she felt so old. Val remembered her mother, who'd called before she left work and said, *"Be careful out in that weather, baby."*

Her mother had called her "baby."

But I'm not a baby. I'm having a baby of my own. But after tomorrow, I won't be pregnant anymore. There's no way I can handle a job and a baby—not without a husband. And I can't go crying home to Mom and Dad. Not after all the things that took place at Christmastime. Everyone's holiday had been ruined—by the police coming to arrest Henry.

Val turned away from the window. The TV blacked out for a moment, before static and lines appeared across the screen, then the picture came on again.

Returning to the couch and her thoughts that wouldn't go away, Val remembered the night she'd conceived her baby. Christmas Eve! She and Henry had made plans for the future, talking about the New Year and how everything was going to be different. But on Christmas Day, the police came. *And now I have no one to plan with. All I can do is let go of the past. Make my own future the best I can—and let Henry make his.*

Of course, Val knew her parents would let her move back in with them. But she just couldn't. They didn't know about the baby. They must never know. After the abortion, she would move in with a couple of girlfriends who lived in Cape Girardeau. She could manage to pay one third of the rent.

Her eyes focused on the fire. It was almost out. There wasn't much wood in the box beside the stove. She would need that in the morning. The wood on the back porch would be soaked, too wet to burn.

She opened her purse and took out the over-the-counter sleeping pills she'd bought today, knowing this would be a difficult night to sleep. She hadn't slept much at all since Henry had begged her not to get rid of the baby . . . and not to divorce him.

Going into the bathroom to take the pill, she remembered hearing that one had to be careful about taking pills or drugs because it could harm the unborn baby. But that didn't matter now. After tomorrow, there wouldn't be any baby.

She stuck a pill into her mouth and swallowed it with water, hoping it would take effect soon. She made her way to the bedroom, switched on a lamp, then returned to the living room.

Ignoring the *bleep-bleep-bleep* warning of severe conditions and the words scrolling across the bottom of the TV giving a weather update, she pushed the "off" button and plunged the room into complete blackness except for the faint red glow of the fire burning low and the dim light at the bedroom doorway.

She shivered, hearing the wind and rain against the windows. The house shook. She took off her tennis shoes, turned down the quilt and blankets, slipped beneath them, and switched off the lamp.

Feeling groggy already, she placed her hand over the spot where the baby was growing. "Oh, Henry," she wailed aloud. "How did things go so wrong?"

But she knew the answer to that. She knew, and Henry knew. She'd ruined both their lives. Henry wouldn't be in prison now if it weren't for her.

It all started with gambling, she admitted. With kids, just having a good time—having plain, innocent fun.

How could such a simple thing get so out of control?

"Gambling," Henry said to Natalie while waiting and hoping for the waters to recede. "It ruined our lives." He told her about his introduction to gambling. He'd had a date with Valerie, the kid sister of Frank Richardson, an SIU college friend and a business and accounting major like himself. He and Frank had known each other in high school. Frank was the son of a bank president and a smart guy, but he didn't care that much about his grades. Henry, on the other hand, was the oldest son of a widowed mother who had four other children. Henry worked summers as a carpenter, saved his money, and even took out a college loan. His and Frank's lifestyles seemed as far apart as the north and south poles.

In college, however, they discovered they had a lot in common. They had several classes together and, during their junior year, worked on a banking project that won national acclaim.

"That's when Frank's dad took notice of me," Henry said, knowing it probably held no interest for this girl, who finally said her name was Natalie and most likely was scared out of her wits. He was! But to try to keep her mind off their situation, he kept talking. Maybe this Natalie could think of him as a person and not a *kidnapper*. He swallowed hard, admitting the reality of what he'd done.

"And that's when I took notice of Val," he said. "She'd just started college in the fall." Henry remembered every detail about her, everything she'd said that evening when he'd gone to the Richardsons' for dinner. It seemed the family had faded into the background as he'd looked across the table into Val's light brown eyes that flashed little golden flecks, into a heart-shaped face surrounded by short dark curls. Her face was animated, and she'd seemed truly excited about his interest in banking, talking about it intelligently. On the other hand, she had traveled abroad, had even spent a summer in Paris studying art. She was an art major, although she lay no claim to being an artist.

"That's when I thought she would never notice me, beyond my being a friend of Frank's. But she liked me," he said, still in awe of that fact. "When I asked her out, she even said, 'I thought you'd never ask.' "

Henry laughed lightly and looked over at Natalie. He thought she might have said something. But she simply nodded slightly as if she were listening to him. Then he realized it must be getting lighter outside for him to be able to see her profile like that. Perhaps his eyes had adjusted more to the darkness, but it did seem the sky might be brightening a little. And the rain didn't sound as heavy.

He turned on the headlights. The water was lower and wasn't moving so fast. The rain had indeed slackened. But the downward slant of the levee in front of them was still covered in water. He'd better wait and hope the whole thing didn't give way before the water receded.

The clock registered 8:35. About twenty or twenty-five minutes before his class at the college would be over. He couldn't know for certain if they'd missed him yet, if the police were out looking for him. He knew the class was having their midterm exam tonight and the instructor might have skipped taking attendance. That would have bought some more time. And he knew the other inmates wouldn't rat on him. Such was the unwritten law in prison. A snitch was about the worst thing an inmate could be. He just hoped the guards weren't paying much attention tonight. If they hadn't yet figured out he was gone, they certainly would when they got back to the prison around nine-thirty and did a head count. He *had* to get to the farmhouse soon and see Val. All this must not be in vain.

A shiver ran through him. There wouldn't already be cops waiting for him at the farmhouse, would there? He shuddered to think of that possibility.

"It's looking better," Henry said, trying to sound confident. He turned off the lights, then continued his story.

"Frank and his date were going with us. Valerie suggested going to the Riverboat."

Henry looked ahead at the rushing water, but in his mind he was looking back to that first date with Val. He'd been pleased that Val had made such a suggestion. It sounded like much more fun than the usual eat-and-see-a-movie kind of date. This was special. Val and Frank had been there before. In fact, Henry later learned that Frank had taken Val there as a sixteenth birthday present. Val had been ecstatic that with the fake ID Frank presented, she had passed for the legal gambling age.

"I was brought up to believe that gambling was a sin," Henry said to Natalie. "But that night, we all had fun. Lost a little, won a little. No big deal. We didn't hurt anyone, not even our own finances. It was just a game, and we all knew how to be sensible about it. How could that be sinful?"

He shook his head. "What I didn't know was that it could get in the blood, become addictive, just as much as alcohol or other drugs. Did you know that?"

Henry suddenly stopped talking. Why was he telling this complete stranger his life story? What did she care? He closed his eyes and, with his elbow on the steering wheel, rested his head in his hand. *I'm sorry, Val. I'm sorry for everything.*

Natalie waited quietly for Henry to go on, but he seemed to be exhausted. She wondered how this escaped prisoner, sitting on top of a levee while floodwaters threatened them, could have such a conversation with her, as if they were friends or something. Perhaps he *was* crazy. But what could she do?

"I've heard that," she said finally.

Henry made a sound like a disgusted snort. "Huh? Heard what?"

"I've heard that gambling can be an addiction," Natalie said. "You were saying—"

"Oh yeah . . ." He looked at her incredulously and laughed. It was as if he'd forgotten she was even there. "Yeah . . . yeah, it can. I know that now. But I didn't believe it then. It's still hard to believe. But when your credit cards are up to the limit because of gambling and you have to start selling your furniture to pay the bills, and you run out of food before payday, then you begin to realize there's much more to this gambling obsession than just a game."

His talking about the addiction to gambling reminded Natalie of Scott's talking about his mother's addiction to alcohol. But Mrs. Lambert was now considered a recovering alcoholic. "People can change," Natalie ventured. "If they let God help them."

She thought he wasn't going to respond. She certainly didn't want to make him angry by mentioning

God . . . but hadn't he asked her to pray just a little while ago?

"God doesn't care about me," Henry said after a long moment. "Not after everything I've done. Every time I try to put things right, I just make them worse. Now I'm about to lose my wife . . . lose our baby. My mom's health is failing because of . . ." He hesitated before adding, ". . . the situation. I just want to talk to Val. Make her listen to reason."

What if Val won't listen? Natalie was thinking. What would Henry do then? What had he done in the past?

She trembled and hugged her arms. It was getting cold in the car, but she didn't want to mention it. She desperately wanted her mom and her family. Suppose she never saw them again? What would this do to her mom, who'd said her children had been a part of her body and were forever a part of her heart?

And why am I thinking these things, she wondered. *I've heard people's lives flash before their eyes before they die. Is that why Henry is talking about his life? Is that why I'm remembering everything and everyone? I really think we might drown in this flood. I know I'm going to heaven if I die, but there's so much I still want to do. Oh, God, is this my time to go? This way?*

Five

What a rush this is! Sean told himself as he hung up the phone and recorded the latest bets in his notebook. His take was going to be sizable for this game—he could feel it—and he began to dream about what he was going to do with all that money. *This is what I call a real education,* Sean laughed to himself. *Not like all that boring textbook stuff.*

He was proud of the new friends he'd made since he'd started his betting service. It had increased his dad's business, too, for a lot of the guys had started coming to the station for their gas. It felt good being popular. He was glad to be out of that drug stuff. He'd known all along that was dangerous. But this—taking bets, making bets, winning a little, losing a little, taking a chance—this was fun. Good, clean fun.

Everybody knew he never bet on his own charts. That way they couldn't accuse him of cheating. Of course, it didn't matter that he had his name on just about every chart in every school except Shawnee High. And he won a lot, too. He knew what Stick Gordon could do!

It made the games more exciting to know you had a price hanging on the score. So what if Stick Gordon ran across that court a hundred times and got the crowd to their feet when he threw those three-pointers?

What difference did it make? Unless you had a few dollars bet on it!

It was close to nine when he sauntered into the Pizza Palace later that evening.

"Hey, Sean," someone called. Sean looked around to see several guys from school in a booth. He and his notebook joined them. He wasn't a loner anymore, working evenings in a food warehouse. He worked with his dad when he wasn't "too busy" with his new business. Everybody knew him now. He bent his wet, blond head over the open notebook while the guys heatedly debated the possible outcome of next week's game. He wrote their names down. They reached into their pockets, then backed up their opinions with hard, cold cash.

The waitress, Phyllis Haney, came over. She and Sean shared a secret grin. She *really* understood the business and didn't fool around with high-school basketball games. She knew where the real money was: in selling lottery tickets to the underaged. In return for her favor, Phyllis helped herself to a percentage of any winnings. At the moment, she had the unspoken monopoly on this little business, but that could change, Sean reminded himself with a grin. Tonight, as soon as everybody cleared out of here, he had business with her.

Yeah, he could forget about his parents' problems. And the fact that Ruthie Ryan had rejected him.

He had really begun to enjoy life.

<hr>

The next time Henry turned on the headlights, both he and Natalie were surprised to see that the rain had almost stopped and the water had gone down enough for them to drive off the levee. Natalie looked at the clock. 8:55 P.M. Her mother's class was just about over. It wouldn't be long now until they knew she was missing and they'd come looking for her.

"The road should be here somewhere," Henry was saying under his breath, leaning forward as he drove. A few yards farther on he exclaimed, "Here it is!" then turned left off the levee and onto an access road leading downward into the valley.

Henry switched on the radio. Flood alerts were being broadcast for the entire area. All roads to Cape Girardeau were closed.

"That's this area, isn't it?" Natalie ventured to ask.

"Yes, but we'll be all right," he said. "I was raised in Cape Girardeau. This access road to the levee has never flooded in my lifetime, and it leads to the farmhouse where my wife and I live. The farmhouse is on a knoll, and Val is the third generation to live in it. Don't worry. You'll be safe."

Don't worry! went through Natalie's mind. *Here I am with an escaped prisoner driving Mom's car. Nobody even knows yet that I'm missing, and the prison may not even know yet that Henry has escaped!* He'd told her he was going to a class at the college—so she knew now that he was a minimum security prisoner. She also knew that the guards could be pretty lax about such prisoners. It was entirely possible that they wouldn't know he was gone until the head count at the prison at ten o'clock. And, added to that, they were in the middle of the most dangerous flood spot in the county. *Don't worry, he says. Suppose his wife isn't at the farmhouse? What will he do then? The authorities will surely be looking for us by that time.*

"You think your wife will be there?" Natalie asked. She wanted to know what to expect. Maybe she'd prefer taking her chances in the storm to being in a farmhouse alone with an escaped prisoner.

"I hope so" was all Henry said.

At nine o'clock, Jill Ainsworth waited at the side door of Logan Junior College, watching classmates leave, one by one. Some hurried to their cars; others were picked up at the door. Soon, everyone would be gone. There were a couple of classes that held until ten o'clock. At least she wasn't alone in the building.

She'd better call Cissy and find out if Natalie had left yet. She went to the office to use the phone.

"She never came, Mrs. Ainsworth," Cissy said. "I thought maybe she changed her mind because of the weather."

"Well, it was raining pretty hard when she dropped me off. Maybe she went to the college library to wait for it to let up."

Jill told herself she wasn't worried, but she heard the anxiety in Cissy's voice. "Have her call me, will you, Mrs. Ainsworth?"

"Yes, I'll tell her."

Jill hung up, trying not to visualize Natalie having been in an accident, or maybe sliding off the wet road into a tree or ditch. "I'll check the library," she said under her breath. Natalie could have gone there and lost track of time. She hurried off down the hall.

The librarian said she hadn't noticed anyone in particular answering Natalie's description—light brown hair, blue eyes, average size. "That could describe a lot of students."

"She's a high-school senior," Jill added.

The librarian smiled, and Jill knew that didn't help. She looked around at several average-looking girls sitting at tables studying. Natalie would have fit right in. The librarian gave her a sympathetic look as Jill started to leave, saying, "She's probably out there waiting for me now." She hadn't looked out in the parking lot yet. She had expected Natalie to pick her up at the door.

This time, Jill set her books down at the doorway

and ventured out into the parking lot to look for their car. It was still raining but lightly now. Only a few cars were left, including the prison bus.

After hurrying back inside, she went to the office again and called home. "Amy," she said to her fifteen-year-old daughter, who'd been left in charge of her two younger sisters. "Has Natalie come back home?" When she heard the answer, she tried to sound unconcerned, not wanting to worry her children. "Well, she's probably doing what I said and driving slowly and carefully. I'm sure she'll show up soon."

When she hung up, the secretary had turned off the computer and was putting away file folders. "Are you leaving soon?" Jill asked her.

"I hope so," the secretary answered. "There are flood watches. The director has gone to the classes to tell them to dismiss early."

"My ride hasn't come yet. It's my daughter. She's never late."

The secretary nodded sympathetically, as had the librarian. "I'll be here for a few more minutes, if you want to use the phone again."

Jill nodded. She called Ruthie Ryan, who lived only a block away from them. Natalie hadn't been there, either, and Ruthie hadn't heard from her. Who else could she call?

Her husband, Jim, was working the evening shift at the prison. There was nothing he could do. Jill then rang the sheriff's office and asked if there had been any accidents between the college and Garden Acres, where Cissy Stiles lived. There'd been none reported, but they would contact patrols with the information.

"Thank you," Jill said. "I'll wait for your call." She hung up with a shaky hand. She should have followed her instincts and insisted Natalie stay home tonight, where she'd be dry and safe. But then she was a good driver, and one couldn't stay home every time the weather was bad, could one? *Yes!* Jill answered her own question. When it was your own child, you could insist.

When the director returned, Jill told him her story and he said the secretary could leave. He'd stay with Jill until they heard something—even drive her home if necessary. "The weather's bad," he said. "A car could stall in all that rain. It's probably no more than that."

"She has a cell phone," Jill replied.

"Have you tried calling her?" he asked.

Jill felt foolish. "I didn't," she admitted and immediately dialed the number. No ring. Apparently, the phone was not turned on.

"Does she have this number?" the director asked when Jill hung up the phone. She knew he was trying not to appear concerned.

"No. But she would have called home if she needed help. I'll check outside again. Maybe she's here now."

"Fine," he said, "and I'll call security."

Jill knew Natalie would have come in the building if she'd arrived late. For now she didn't know what else to do but go to the doorway and peer out into the dark night.

It seemed like forever until the police called the college office and spoke to her. They'd only found two minor accidents on the highway, and neither answered the description of her car or her daughter.

The college security guard came in. He'd found no sign of a stranded car on campus and did not recall seeing the car.

Just then a correctional officer from the prison stepped into the office. Jill recognized him. It was good to see a familiar face. He might know what to do. "Carl," she said with some relief.

"Mrs. Ainsworth?" Carl Sisk questioned, as if he hardly recognized her, and she suddenly realized she must look like a wet washrag. But that hardly mattered!

"Sorry, I can't talk right now," he said, looking as worried as she felt. Then he addressed the director and security officer. Carl's next words wrenched her heart and terrified her beyond reason. "The premises need to be searched. I have a prisoner missing."

What will I do if Val isn't there? Henry kept asking himself. His only thought before he'd planned this escape was to get to Val. He'd take a car. Nobody would get hurt. He'd be charged with car theft and escape. But it would be worth it, just to make Val listen to him. And it would be in the papers. Her parents refused to have any contact with him. Someone who knew them would read about the escape in the papers, even if the Richardsons didn't, and make them listen to his reason for this. Although his own life was ruined, maybe he could save the life of his unborn child. He could not sit by and let his child be destroyed.

But he hadn't counted on the storm, the rain, or the floodwaters. And he hadn't counted on taking anyone with him. Now he'd also be charged with kidnapping. He shuddered to think how many years that would add to his sentence. And now he had an added responsibility to keep the girl safe. Otherwise, he'd never get out of prison. He'd be charged with murder!

The weight of the situation, and the fear that Val would not be at the farmhouse, settled upon him like a boulder on his chest. When he'd embezzled from his in-laws' bank, he'd done it for what he thought was a good reason. He was just trying to protect Val—not let her parents know about her gambling problem and the terrible debt they were in because of it. But it hadn't solved anything. It had only made things worse.

And this escape. Henry meant well again. He

wanted to make Val change her mind about getting rid of the baby. Instead, he was endangering this girl's life and his own. If they both drowned, nobody would ever know his real intentions. And instead of saving his baby's life, he'd be taking a young girl's.

Oh, God! he prayed. *I keep messing up. I don't know if you'll even listen to me, but for the girl's sake, please don't let her die. She's done nothing wrong. Please don't let her die.*

Henry's apprehensions grew as he realized the water was higher up on this road than he'd ever known it to be. Soon, however, he'd be off the access road and onto the narrow wooden bridge stretching over the lowest section of the farmland. Then he'd be on the road leading up to the farmhouse on the knoll.

It was just raining lightly now, and the wind had abated. But he knew the floodwaters were still a danger. They'd be safe at the farmhouse, though, whether or not Val was there. They had to be.

He strained to see a light that might be shining from a window, but he saw nothing in the black night. Then as the road curved, the headlights shone on Val's car, parked at the side of the little house.

"That's her car," he told Natalie. "Come on. Go up on the porch."

With Henry right behind her, Natalie sloshed through the water standing on the narrow gravel walkway, up to the front porch, and held on to the banister while Henry tried the door. It was locked.

He knocked loudly. No response.

"Val!" he called. No answer.

"Maybe she left with somebody," he said. *Or maybe she's already had the abortion*, he thought, *and is inside, too weak to answer the door. But maybe she's had second thoughts—*

"I've got to get inside," he said. "You stay here." He ran off and disappeared around the corner of the house.

Where would I go? Natalie asked silently as she waited on the porch. *He has the car keys.* Maybe she should look around for something to hit him with. Surprise him when he came back, then get the car keys and drive back down that road and return the way they'd come. That would mean she'd have to leave him unconscious here at the farmhouse. Could she just leave him here to die?

Then a worse thought occurred to her. What if he were lying about his wife? Maybe he had no wife. Or at least not here. Maybe this was an abandoned farmhouse.

She didn't know what to believe, and before she could even decide what to do, she heard a vehicle coming, then suddenly she was engulfed in the lights of the car.

A momentary sense of relief flooded her. Was it the police? Was she rescued? She turned from the headlights and saw Henry, looking as surprised as she felt, standing with the front door open. Apparently, Henry had found a door or window unlocked, or had broken in and come through the house.

Then the car lights were off and a man was running toward them, a flashlight bobbing in his hand. "Henry?" he shouted, just as Henry said, "Frank?"

This must be Henry's brother-in-law he'd been telling her about. He hadn't sounded too bad when Henry told the story, but this Frank was clearly angry. He bounded up on the porch beside her, looking and acting as if he were full of hate.

Here she was in the middle of nowhere. In the middle of a flooded, evacuated area, at the mercy of two men now, instead of just one. One thought dominated all others in Natalie's mind, as if she had suddenly reverted to her childhood: *Mom*, her entire being seemed to wail. *I want my mom!*

Six

Jill listened intently to Officer Carl Sisk as he called the message center at the federal prison. "We have a missing inmate," he reported and gave what information he had.

Yes, he'd had a count and name check as the inmates entered the building and watched as they all went into the advanced computer course classroom. He'd marked the time: 5:54 P.M.

No, the instructor didn't recall having seen Henry Miller, but he hadn't taken roll call since the students were having their midterm computer exam. There'd been students arriving late because of the bad weather, and some leaving early when their tests were completed. Any inmate finishing early could have left the classroom without anyone questioning it.

Jill was startled by this last comment. *Where was Carl—and the other guard—during class?* she wondered. *Wouldn't they have noticed a prisoner leaving early?* She couldn't help feeling angry now about such lax security. Due to the guards' lack of caution, her daughter might be out there right now with one of these men they were supposed to be guarding!

The other inmates claimed to know nothing, Carl was explaining into the phone. Jill knew that was the code in a prison—no snitching!

"I have some other information that may be significant," Carl added. "A seventeen-year-old girl was supposed to pick her mother up at nine. Maybe she's running late, but we have to consider the worst. If there's a connection here, then Miller might have taken her and her car at either a couple minutes past six or before nine when she came to pick up her mother. And you'll never believe this," he added ominously. "The girl is none other than the daughter of senior officer specialist, Jim Ainsworth."

Carl was nodding with the phone receiver to his ear, his expression very troubled. "Yes, sir. I'll get the other prisoners back immediately."

He hung up the phone and turned to Jill. "I can't tell you how sorry I am about this, Mrs. Ainsworth. We'll do everything we can to locate your daughter. All local, county, and state patrols are being alerted right now, as well as the FBI and the U.S. Marshall's office. They'll search the campus here and set up road blocks at any possible escape routes."

"Thank you, Carl," Jill said, trying not to let her anger show. She and Jim had known Carl a long time, and she wanted to give him the benefit of the doubt, not jump to hasty conclusions. "I know you'll do everything possible. Does Jim know yet?"

"Yes, they're sending an officer to relieve him right now so he can come home to be with you. And I've called for a squad car to take you home. They should be here any minute. Meanwhile, I've got to get the prisoners back to the prison—pronto! We don't want the rest of them getting any ideas."

Jill fought back tears and tried to steady her voice as she asked, "Do you think this man would try to hurt my daughter, Carl?"

Carl put his hand on Jill's shoulder. "I can't tell you for sure, but we can hope that he simply wants to get away. Henry Miller isn't a bad man as far as I can tell—he was a model prisoner, and we all trusted him. He would have been out on parole very shortly if he'd kept up his good behavior. I'm as surprised as anyone that Miller would pull a stunt like this. And we have to remember, we don't know for certain that Natalie is with him. Maybe she's run into car trouble and we'll find her along the highway. Let's hope so."

Carl started to leave the office, then turned and faced Jill again. "I promise you, Mrs. Ainsworth, I personally will not sleep until we find your daughter."

As Sisk turned on his heel and went out the door, Jill could see through the glass windows that the promised squad car was already pulling up at the side entrance for her.

At the federal prison, Jim Ainsworth was supervising several junior officers as they kept watch on the inmates' basketball game. Tempers could flare easily in these competitive games, but it also served to work off a lot of pent-up energy. Glancing up at the big clock on the wall, Jim felt a sense of relief that after lockup and the head count, he could go home to his family.

He didn't mind at all when Officer Whyte came in and said Lieutenant Landry wanted to see him. He had a good working and personal relationship with Landry. They were on the same prison bowling team.

But his smile faded when he walked into Landry's office. He could tell by the lieutenant's face that something big was up.

"Sit down, Jim," Landry said, motioning to the chair opposite his desk. At first, news of the escape didn't bother Jim too much, since Landry emphasized that Miller had no previous record, was minimum security, and was in prison for embezzling from a bank.

Miller said he'd done it to pay taxes so the IRS wouldn't put a lien on the house he was living in that belonged to his wife's parents. "Because her parents had already been generous," Landry explained. "Miller was too embarrassed to go to them and ask for money."

Jim huffed and shook his head. Pride and embarrassment caused him to steal? He'd rather chance going to jail? But then, criminals didn't expect to get caught. They thought they were too smart for the police. But the prison was full of them!

"He's been a model prisoner during his three-month incarceration," continued the lieutenant.

Jim wondered why Landry was going into so much detail about this. The procedure for this kind of escape was routine. Had Miller been maximum security and escaped from the institution, then all available officers would be called in. Jim himself had pursued an escapee out into the dark, cold night on foot.

It wasn't until Landry said Miller had gone to his class at Logan Junior College that Jim felt an uneasiness. His wife had a class tonight at Logan.

"We think he took somebody's car. We don't know if that was around six or nine P.M., but most likely six."

Jim cleared his throat. A car? Well, cars could be replaced.

"And, Jim, we think he might have taken a hostage."

Jim was leaning forward now, his hands on the chair arms. "Not . . . Jill? Landry! What are you saying?"

"No," Landry said, taking a deep breath and looking up toward the ceiling. "Not your wife."

"Whew!" Jim exhaled loudly. "You had me scared. I don't care if he took her car." Seeing Landry's pained expression, Jim leaned forward again. "She wasn't hurt, was she, Lan? Jill wouldn't try to fight anyone for a car."

"Jim . . . your daughter drove your wife to her class."

Jim was on his feet then. "Natalie? He took Natalie?"

"We don't know, Jim. There's been no report of an accident. We can only assume that Miller took your wife's car." He swallowed hard. "And Natalie, too."

"I'm going after him!" Jim stormed. Not bothering to ask permission, he reached over and grabbed Miller's files in front of Landry and began to read.

"I've read the files, Jim," Landry said. "Miller's wife recently filed for divorce. You know this kind of thing tears an inmate up. No doubt he's headed for his home."

Jim was frantic. He had to get out of there. Find his daughter. "But why take Natalie?"

Landry shook his head. "You know the answer, Jim."

Jim nodded. He knew. If an inmate wanted to get away, he'd do anything to accomplish it.

"I'm going after him," Jim shouted again, jumping up and heading for the door.

"No, Jim." Landry caught Jim's arm and forcibly drew him back into the office. "You're needed at home. You know what you'd say to any other officer if this happened to him."

"Sure, I do," Jim replied. "But wouldn't you go if it was your daughter?"

Landry looked down at the desk. "Look, Jim. We've already alerted the authorities. They're out there right now combing the area. There's nothing more you can do. You go home to your wife and daughters. They need you more. I'll keep you informed of our every move."

"Okay, I'll go home," Jim finally conceded. "But I'll be back. If Henry Miller's got my daughter—"

"He just wants to get home, Jim," Landry said.

Jim nodded. That's what he'd said before, too. In the almost twenty years he'd worked for the federal prison system, he'd made those routine statements plenty of times. Sometimes things turned out all right. Sometimes . . . they didn't.

Jim hurriedly left the prison and made his way to his car. As the gates opened to let him out, he switched on the radio and began hearing reports of widespread flooding. He had been in the prison all day and had not realized how much rain there'd been. He turned to the local radio station to hear the weather report. His nightmare grew worse when the reporter said that all roads down toward Cape Girardeau were closed or flooded. There was a flood watch posted all along the Mississippi and surrounding areas. They feared the levees wouldn't hold.

The focus of his fear suddenly turned from Natalie being at the mercy of Henry Miller to the even more dangerous possibility that she could be somewhere near the deadly floodwaters of the raging Mississippi.

Seven

Jill Ainsworth's call to Cissy was like throwing a wet blanket on her party. She sensed something was terribly wrong. "Natalie hasn't shown up at the college," she said to her friends, worried. "Maybe we'd better break this up and you guys call me when you get home. I hate to think of any of you stranded out there in that downpour."

They all laughed uneasily, agreeing that they'd better go, and congratulated Cissy again. But concern was on each of their faces as they headed toward the front of the house.

Katlyn hung back while the other girls gathered in the foyer and collected their coats and umbrellas from Cornelia.

"What do you suppose happened, Cissy?" Katlyn asked, her eyes as dark as her long black hair. Even Katlyn, jealous as she was over Scott and Natalie's relationship, certainly didn't want Natalie stranded out in the storm.

"A flat tire? Maybe she even slid off the road in weather like this." Cissy shrugged helplessly yet tried to look on the bright side. "Maybe she realized there was something else she had to do—or she stopped to help someone—and is just running late."

Katlyn nodded. They all knew Natalie was that

way. She'd even been there to help Katlyn, even though Katlyn hadn't always been very kind to Natalie. "I hope she's okay," Katlyn said sincerely.

Cissy nodded. "Oh, she's probably at the college by now. You know how moms are. They always worry."

Katlyn agreed and headed for her waiting raincoat. "Call me when you find out anything."

"I will," Cissy promised.

Cissy had just turned toward her mother's private sitting room when Elizabeth Stiles walked toward her. "Have your guests left already, dear?"

"Yes, Mom. We might have a problem."

Elizabeth's sky blue eyes, mirroring Cissy's, immediately turned sympathetic. "I thought it was early for one of your parties to end—even this impromptu one."

"It's Natalie. I expected her around six, but she didn't come. Her mom just called and said Natalie was to pick her up at nine at Logan Junior College, but she's not there yet."

Elizabeth looked at her wristwatch. "It's not even nine-thirty yet. With all the rain, she'd have to drive slowly."

"But, Mom, you know it's not like Natalie to be late or not show up without calling."

"Yes, I do," her mother admitted. "No one is more dependable than Natalie Ainsworth." Her lovely face brightened then. "But you know, if she came upon someone in trouble, she would do what she could to summon help for them. Or if children were involved, she'd even stop to help."

Cissy nodded. "But we have to make sure, Mom."

"Yes, darling, I know. I'll just bet your next call to the Ainsworths will find Natalie and Jill safe at home."

"Probably," Cissy agreed. "But, Mom, I feel so selfish. I was so excited about sharing my great news that I hardly gave Natalie a second thought after she didn't show up. I even dragged my friends out in this miserable weather. Oh, Mom! Maybe I haven't changed so much after all."

"Now, Cissy, stop blaming yourself. You don't know that anything bad has happened. And you know your friends would be disappointed if you didn't share your good news with them as soon as possible. You know they'd do the same."

Cissy nodded. "I meant well, and I know Natalie would be pleased that a Christian company contacted me. But I was on that ego trip again." She lowered her eyes and shook her head. "I feel really bad, Mom. Natalie has changed my whole life—my whole attitude toward the most important things in life."

Elizabeth put her arm around her daughter's shoulder and looked at her warmly. "She's changed all our lives, Cissy. She is one of those dear people who just seem to have a closer walk with God than many of us. He's with her, you know."

"Yes, I know," she admitted. "But I'm supposed to be her friend. What kind of person forgets her own friend when she's out in a storm?"

"Cissy, if it will make you feel better, I'll have your father check the hospital to see if there's been an accident. But first, let's give them time to get home."

"In the meantime, I can do what Natalie would do," Cissy said. "Pray!"

Cissy waited until 9:45 to call the Ainsworths. *They should be home by now*, she thought, *even driving slowly*.

Natalie's sister Amy answered the phone. "They're not home yet," she said in a concerned voice. "Mom called to ask if Natalie came back home after dropping her off at the college, but she didn't. We thought she was at your house."

"She didn't come, Amy. I guess I should have let someone know—"

"Well, Mom said for me to stay off the phone in case Natalie calls—oh, wait a minute. I hear a car."

Amy soon came back to the phone, out of breath and talking fast. "It's the police! They just brought Mom home, and Natalie's not with her. I gotta go."

Cissy heard the click in her ear. *The police!*

Cissy laid the receiver down and turned to face her parents. The three of them were now in her dad's study. The gas fireplace was turned on, giving the impression of a cozy log-burning fire. "Dad?" she pleaded. "Amy says the police just brought her mother home . . . and Natalie wasn't with her."

John Stiles rose from his recliner at once. "I'll contact the hospitals," he said.

As a hospital administrator, her dad could get more information, and more quickly, than the ordinary person about anyone admitted to the hospital.

But just then a special news report came on the TV. This time it was not about the weather and flooding conditions, but about an escaped prisoner—and the possibility that he may have stolen a car and kidnapped a seventeen-year-old girl.

The Stileses stood transfixed, watching and listening. The report gave the name and a description of Henry Miller, but not of the girl, pending further investigation.

"Mom," Cissy whispered unbelievingly, "I have to go to the Ainsworths'."

Cissy saw the change take place on her mother's face. Her protests that she wanted to make turned to acceptance. She couldn't say, "Don't go out in that nasty weather." Natalie had braved tornado warnings for Cissy. If Natalie was in trouble—how could any of them not try to help?

Cissy was ready to go by the time her dad finished making his calls. "Nothing," he said. "No one fitting Natalie's description has been taken to any area hospitals."

"Then she's out there somewhere," Cissy said.

"We don't know that the kidnapped girl is Natalie," her mom said, trying to be encouraging.

"We don't know that it's not," Cissy rebutted. "Should I call Scott?"

"No," Elizabeth said.

John added, "Not until we know something definite."

"I'll call Helen and Lawrence," Elizabeth said, speaking of Scott's parents. "And Aunt Martha. We'll start a prayer chain."

Cissy felt good about the prayer chain, especially if it were led by her mom's older sister, Martha Brysen. If anyone knew how to pray, Aunt Martha sure did! At the same time, Cissy kept wishing she'd done something three hours earlier, after Natalie had not showed up at her house.

It was not raining as much now as it had been earlier, but the wind was still blowing hard, and water stood on the road in huge puddles. Cissy had to switch lanes frequently to avoid going through the standing water.

As she neared the Ainsworths' house, she saw a police car parked on the street. It looked as if every light in the neighboring homes was on. Cissy pulled into the Ainsworths' driveway.

Ruthie Ryan opened the door even before Cissy plodded up the walkway to the small stoop at the front of the house. "It's just Cissy," Ruthie called over her shoulder to those inside the house.

"Have they heard anything?" Cissy asked immediately.

"Nothing at all. Mrs. A said Natalie had planned to go to *your* house," Ruthie said as Cissy closed her umbrella and piled it against others on the stoop, somewhat protected by an overhang. She felt sure Ruthie's statement was an accusation. That girl had a way of speaking her mind.

"Don't get on my case, Ruthie," Cissy pleaded, stepping past her onto a throw rug that had been placed at the doorway in the living room. "I feel completely rotten about inviting Natalie out on a night like this." She shucked out of her drippy raincoat and held it out to Ruthie.

"You can put your coat in the bathroom. There are hangers on the shower curtain rod," Ruthie informed her, with an expression that seemed to say she wasn't about to wait hand and foot on Cissy Stiles.

My faux pas, Cissy was thinking. She had assumed Ruthie was helping with coats. She should have known Ruthie wouldn't help with hers anyway.

After hanging her coat in the bathroom, Cissy looked around the small living room. She recognized the Ryan family—Ruthie's mom, dad, and little brother. Also the preacher and his wife from the church the Ainsworths attended. She had seen some of the others but didn't know their names. A couple of young people from Natalie's youth group appeared at the doorway and stepped in behind Cissy.

"Word's gotten around quickly," Ruthie said. "The phone's been ringing off the hook."

Cissy spied Mrs. Ainsworth then and headed toward her. "I'm so sorry, Mrs. Ainsworth, that I didn't call someone after Natalie didn't show up at my house."

"Don't blame yourself, Cissy," said Jill. "I shouldn't have let Natalie go out on a night like this. Then it would have been me who's missing, rather than Natalie."

Cissy felt helpless as Jill took a deep, shaky breath

and stared at the phone as it began to ring.

Ruthie took Cissy's arm and led her into the kitchen. The young people followed—Natalie's three younger sisters, Ruthie's brother, and several kids from the neighborhood. They sat around the table after some accepted Amy's offer of drink and cookies.

"No, thanks," Cissy replied and glanced at Ruthie, who then asked how her party went.

"Fine, but I wish now I hadn't invited anyone out tonight. It was impulsive."

She had difficulty meeting Ruthie's gaze, wondering if Ruthie blamed her for Natalie's disappearance.

Then Ruthie said contritely, "I keep thinking that maybe this wouldn't have happened if I'd accepted your invitation. Nat and I could have gone together. Now studying for a test seems unimportant." She shrugged helplessly and Cissy saw the moisture gathering in her eyes.

"That's hindsight, Ruthie," Cissy said. "We just can't know the future."

Ruthie nodded. "Don't blame yourself, either." She inhaled deeply and squared her shoulders. "Now, what was your good news?"

All eyes focused on Cissy, as they had at her home earlier. This time it was different. It would surely sound like bragging. "Like you said, Ruthie. Things lose their importance when something bigger comes along."

Natalie's thirteen-year-old sister, Sarah, urged them on. "Maybe we shouldn't be thinking the worst. We've all prayed, and I guess we still are on the inside. I'm sure Natalie's going to walk in any minute, and this whole thing will just be a big mistake. Let's get our minds off of it and hear Cissy's news."

"Yeah," others agreed, as if the burden of Natalie's being missing was too great a load to bear.

"I don't want to sound self-centered," Cissy said.

"We won't take it that way," Ruthie assured her. "If you tell your news, I'll tell mine."

Seeing the sudden light dispel the moisture in Ruthie's eyes, Cissy smiled. Yes, maybe they should get their minds on other things.

They all listened intently as Cissy told how the Lord was working in her life and how she would have a greater opportunity now to witness to her faith than if she'd been the top finalist in that modeling search. She didn't fail to mention how Natalie had been a great influence on her growth as a Christian. As quickly as she could, Cissy focused attention on Ruthie. "Now, what's your news, Ruthie?"

"Well, I wrote a paper last month about boyfriend abuse and how it can escalate from verbal to physical."

Cissy nodded her understanding. She knew Ruthie had had trouble with her steady boyfriend around Christmastime, and that's one reason Cissy had invited Ruthie to her home tonight. She herself had experienced boyfriend troubles in the past and thought she might be able to encourage Ruthie.

"Natalie said I should send it to a teen magazine. So I did."

"And?" Cissy encouraged, hoping she knew the rest.

Ruthie appeared astounded as she revealed, "They want to publish it!"

"Wow! That's fantastic, Ruthie."

Amy's mouth flew open. "Are they going to pay you for it?"

Ruthie nodded. "Yep. I signed a contract."

"That makes you a professional writer," Amy gushed.

"Well, not exactly. But it's a start."

"I didn't know you were interested in writing," Cissy said admiringly.

"I've always liked writing papers for English class,

and I like writing in my journal. Maybe it's just wishful thinking, but now I'm excited about trying to be a real writer."

Everyone was obviously impressed.

Just then someone stumbled into the kitchen and caught hold of the doorframe. Stick Gordon, Shawnee High's basketball star, who'd been offered several college scholarships but who was still clumsy off the courts, stood sopping wet and dripping all over the floor.

"Stick!" Amy chided. "Go to the bathroom and dry off!"

He strode into the kitchen and pulled out a chair and flopped down. "I'm not moving a muscle until I know what's going on here."

Then Cissy noticed that his quick glance at Ruthie caused his ears to turn red and Ruthie to glance away. Every time Cissy had been around Ruthie and Stick in the past, they'd been at each other's throats. This sudden shyness was something new. Cissy smiled to herself. *Is there something going on here I haven't heard about?*

Eight

"Where's Val? What have you done to her now?" Frank was shouting at Henry and waving the flashlight at him. Natalie shrank back against the wall of the house, trying to keep out of his way. The man terrified her.

"I don't know," Henry said. "I just got here. I climbed through a kitchen window. The power's off."

"I know that," Frank spat. "All the lines are down, and the water's rising fast. Where's my sister?"

"She didn't answer when I came through the house calling her name," Henry said, putting his hands up to shade his eyes from Frank's flashlight. "I don't think she's here."

"She left Mom and Dad's around five. Her car's outside. What have you and your girlfriend here done to her?" He turned the flashlight on Natalie then, and she squinted against the light. "Don't bother to answer," he added vehemently. "I'll deal with you later."

He shoved Henry aside, slamming him up against the door, and shined the light around the living room.

Natalie was shocked that he referred to her as Henry's girlfriend. What would he do if he found out the truth?

"The woodstove's hot," Frank said. "She's here. What did you do, Henry?"

"I told you—" Henry began.

"Don't tell me anything," Frank interrupted. "It would be lies anyway."

Natalie stood at the front door watching as Frank walked farther into the house, shining the light alternately around the room and back on Henry, as if to ensure Henry didn't jump him.

Then she realized that Frank probably left the keys in his vehicle. Maybe she could get to it and drive away. But would both of them come after her in her own car? Would they stay here and fight or gang up on her? She had to try it. She'd put the vehicle in neutral and ease back down the drive. Maybe it would be a while before they realized she was gone.

Just as she started to turn, she heard both men frantically shout, "Val, Val!" Natalie froze and listened. It sounded as if they were trying to awaken Val, to no avail. Natalie heard Frank yell, "Did you drug her, Henry?"

Henry was trying to reason with Frank. At the realization that another woman was here at the mercy of these men, Natalie put aside her thoughts of escape. Whether it was a sense of compassion or fear that compelled her, Natalie wasn't sure, but she quietly tiptoed to the bedroom doorway to see what was happening. Was the woman all right? The flashlight was now on the bed, shining on Frank, who was holding a woman against his chest, but she just moaned and hung her head limply.

"Henry's telling the truth," Natalie said. "We just got here."

Startled, Frank looked toward her. "How can I believe you, any more than I believe him?"

"I kidnapped her, Frank," Henry admitted. "That's her car out there. I had no other way to get here."

"It's true," Natalie said, knowing she had blown any chance of escaping now.

Frank looked at Natalie in disbelief, then back at

Henry. The shadowy light on his face revealed a look of utter contempt. "You . . ." he breathed at Henry. "Why, I oughta—"

"Val could've taken something," Henry said suddenly, grabbing the flashlight to look around on the bedside table and the dresser; then he stepped into the bathroom and came back. "Here's a bottle of sleeping pills. It's almost full."

Henry had succeeded in getting Frank's attention off of him and back on to Val. Frank stood up and lifted the uncooperative Val into his arms. "I've got to get her out of here," he said, but Val had begun to flail her arms and mutter that she wanted to sleep.

Henry came over to help, but Frank ordered him to stay away.

"Wha. . . ? Put me down," Val ordered, squirming in Frank's arms. About to lose his grip, he dropped her on the bed, and she lay down again, trying to pull up the covers.

"Did you take sleeping pills?" Frank demanded to know.

"Mmm-hmm," she mumbled with her eyes closed.

"How many, Val? How many?" Frank yelled frantically.

"One," she said, irritated, and let out a long sigh.

"I'll stay with her," Frank said. "Get out of here."

"I can't do that, Frank. She's pregnant. That's why I came here. To talk some sense into her. She's planning to have an abortion."

"No-o-o-o," Val moaned and tried to pull the covers over her head.

Frank jumped up and lunged for Henry. He dropped the flashlight, and it rolled into the corner, shining against the wall and plunging the room into darkness. Natalie heard one of them being slammed up against something, then someone grunting as if the breath was knocked out of him. She heard Henry gasp. "You've got to help her, Frank," he pleaded. "Don't let her harm the baby."

"I can understand her not wanting *your* baby," Frank ground out.

"Please, Frank. It's hers, too. Don't let her murder the baby."

"And what do you call what you've done to Val?" Frank growled. "You had every chance, Henry. We treated you like family. Dad gave you a job at the bank." His voice became deadly. "And he gave you his only daughter. My sister! Now you come here with this girlfriend of yours. What are you trying to do? Finish the job on Val?"

Natalie felt she had to set Frank straight. She grabbed the flashlight off the floor and aimed it in his direction, revealing that he had Henry backed up against the wall, and Henry's mouth was bleeding. "I'm not his girlfriend!" she shouted. "I never saw him before tonight."

Frank looked dazed. He gazed at her, although he couldn't possibly see beyond the glow of the light, then back at Henry.

Henry confirmed it. "I told you—I kidnapped her, Frank. It was the only way to get here."

Frank gave Henry a final shove, and his head thudded against the wall. Frank went back to the bed. "I've got to get Val out of here. Away from you. And no way can I believe this story. You're stupid, Henry. But surely not stupid enough to kidnap a girl and bring her here. Maybe you just think I'm stupid enough to believe it."

"It's true," Natalie repeated.

"She's a liar, too," Val said groggily from the bed. "Now, leave me alone!"

"No, I'm not lying," Natalie insisted. "I dropped my mom off at Logan Junior College at six o'clock.

That's when Henry got in the car and . . . and brought me here."

"Likely story!" Frank snorted. "If you've been kidnapped, why aren't you screaming bloody murder or running for your life? Why didn't you ask for help when I got here?"

"I was too scared," Natalie admitted. "I thought you might . . ." She paused, not certain how much she dared to say. "Might have planned this together. And all this seems so unreal."

Frank shook his head, then ran his fingers through his hair. "That I can agree with."

"Frank," Henry said. "Listen to me. Val needs your help. She's in trouble. Gambling is an obsession with her. It's ruined our lives, Frank. It means more to her than anything—more than me, her family, even . . ." he rasped out, "even more than our baby."

"No! No!" Val screamed, sitting upright on the bed. "Why are you saying that? You must really hate me, Henry."

"I love you, Val. You know that," Henry said softly. "That's why I came here tonight. You said you were never going to see me again . . . and you were going to get rid of our baby. I wanted to make you listen to reason . . . and tell your parents. They'll help you, Val. They love you, too."

"They won't if you tell them that . . . lie!" Her lips trembled. "I know how much they hate you. The awful things they said about you at the trial. I know how they feel about you."

Frank came closer to the bed and snarled at Henry. "I suppose she did the embezzling, too!"

"No. I . . . I borrowed that . . ."

"Borrowed!" Frank sneered.

"Okay, I stole it," Henry admitted. "I thought I could repay it before anyone knew. I believed Val when she swore she'd change. I didn't realize then that she couldn't. She's addicted, Frank."

Val covered her face and began to sob.

Frank sat on the edge of the bed, alternately staring at Henry, then at his sister, as if they were both strangers. "Tell me this is just another one of his lies, Val."

"Why don't you just haul off and hit me, too, Frank?" Val choked. "I begged you and Dad to take it easy on Henry. But, no, you wanted to throw him in jail. I couldn't stand the fact that all of you would hate me if you knew the truth . . . like you hate Henry." She fell back onto the bed and buried her face in a pillow.

"Are you saying," Frank asked incredulously, "that he's telling the truth? Val, are you . . . you're addicted to . . . gambling?"

"What difference does it make now?" she screamed and jumped to her feet, away from the light, the effects of the sleeping pill apparently worn off now. "Henry will spend his life in jail. I can't handle my own life. How could I manage a baby? Just . . . go away. All of you!"

"No, Val. We've got to get you out of here," Frank said. "The flooding is bad. We aren't safe, even here. If the levee gives, we're all in big trouble."

"I'm not going anywhere," she said and started for the bathroom.

Henry blocked the way.

Frank grabbed her arms from behind.

She began to sob. "Leave me alone. I just want to die."

"You're going, Val. You and I can make it in the Bronco. Step into your house slippers here."

Natalie felt like they'd forgotten about her. "You'll take me with you, won't you?" she asked. Strangers that they were, anything was better than being left alone in the dark, with the icy fingers of rising water creeping ever closer.

Sean felt good about himself every time one of his high-school buddies placed a bet. The winner would be the one closest to the final score. Only a couple of times had more than one guy hit an exact score, so Sean always made more money than he paid out.

That's why he'd made the biggest bet of his career a couple of days ago with Tim Franklin, the guy from Carbondale High who handled the betting for his school. Tim was pretty confident about their new star player and the fact his school had won most of their games this season. But Sean was more confident in Stick Gordon. So confident, in fact, that he'd wagered one hundred dollars on the score and decided to go further. He didn't consider it a gamble, but a sure thing, when he told Franklin, "Bet you two hundred that Stick will shoot and hit three three-pointers."

Even if he lost on the score, he'd double the two hundred. Stick had never let him down yet.

"Why the happy face?" Phyllis asked when everyone else had cleared out.

He grinned. "Oh, just thinking about that book report that's due next week. You got it?"

"Sure," she said, her smile as wide as his. She held out her palm and Sean reluctantly fished into his pocket for his few remaining dollars and dropped them into her hand. The phone rang, and she went to answer it.

"Ruthie," she said, surprised, and Sean knew she'd said the name for his benefit.

His heart did a quick flip-flop, as if Ruthie were still his girlfriend and was calling for him. He was going to win her back. But so far, Ruthie still claimed she didn't love him anymore.

"No, Natalie hasn't been here," Phyllis was saying. "Um, no, it's about closing time and most everybody's gone." She paused, and Sean nodded that it was okay to say he was there. "Just Sean," she said, then held out the receiver to him.

Ruthie wanted to talk to him? Well, it was about time!

He took the receiver and tried to steady his voice when he said, "What's up?"

He could hardly believe what Ruthie was telling him—that Natalie hadn't come home from taking her mom to college and they thought she might have been abducted by an escaped prisoner!

"I'll look along the sides of the roads for their car on my way home," Sean promised.

"Be careful," Ruthie said, probably the most caring thing she'd said since they'd broken up. Then she added, "The reports say that a lot of roads have several inches of water standing on them. Schools are closed tomorrow since the buses can't run on some of the low-lying streets."

Sean was trying to keep his mind on Natalie. What could have happened? Surely she couldn't really have been taken by a prisoner! "Maybe somebody at the college needed a ride and she took them home," he suggested.

"Yeah, that's possible," Ruthie said. "We're hoping and praying for the best, Sean. All the members of the youth group are being called and asked to pray."

He knew that was a roundabout invitation to join them in prayer. He wasn't too big on prayer himself, but he meant it when he said, "I hope she's found and everything's okay, Ruthie."

"Yeah," she said. "I gotta get off the phone."

When Sean told Phyllis the news, she was clearly shocked. "That's unreal," she said, shaking her head. "It's hard to believe something like that could happen to someone you know."

"Yeah," Sean replied. His excitement over his sure bet was suddenly dampened by the chilling possibility that Natalie Ainsworth could be in serious danger.

Phyllis looked around. "If the schools are already closed for tomorrow, the roads must be really bad. I gotta get this place cleaned up and closed up."

"I'll help," Sean said and headed for a booth while Phyllis turned toward the kitchen.

Suddenly, his eyes fastened on a five-dollar bill in the back booth. He remembered a middle-aged couple who'd sat there. Sean stacked the dishes and looked toward the kitchen. No Phyllis in sight. He'd just given the last of the guys' betting money to Phyllis for that book report. He'd just borrow the five. He picked it up and shoved it into his pocket.

She charged too much for those book reports anyway. They were no skin off her teeth. She'd never erased them off her computer. He felt a twinge of conscience, knowing that youth group crowd would call it cheating. But writing his own book reports wasn't going to help him get ahead in life—graduating from high school in a couple of months would!

He found two one-dollar bills on another table and was whistling as he took the dishes into the kitchen and handed her the money.

"Thanks. Rainy-day tips!" she exclaimed with a shake of head, but she was smiling.

He smiled back. Yep, when he won his bundle, he might go on to bigger things. Maybe Ruthie Ryan would take another look at him then!

Nine

"Natalie hasn't been at the Pizza Parlor," Ruthie said after she hung up the phone. "Only ones there are Phyllis and . . . Sean."

Stick thought he wasn't the only one who noticed Ruthie's voice quiver when she said "Sean." They all looked at her with concern. Was it because Natalie wasn't at the Pizza Parlor or because Ruthie's heart was breaking? After all, she'd gone steady with Sean for a couple of years.

Ruthie ducked her head, but now that she had that cool short haircut, the hair didn't hide her face like it used to. Someone had to say something. They had been laughing and talking when he'd come in—maybe he wouldn't be out of line to joke around now.

"Say, what was that you said about a spider when I came in?" he asked as if serious. "Lead me to it. I'll smash it!" He pounded his chest like Tarzan.

Well, at least he got Ruthie's little brother, Justin, to crack up. A few giggled, but most looked at him as if he was some kind of nut—as usual.

It was Cissy who answered. "*Writer*, not spider," she said. "I guess you'll just have to stomp Ruthie. She's the one."

Smart move, Stick! He'd tried to get their attention off Ruthie and now it was right back on her. So much for good intentions.

Ruthie's mom breezed into the kitchen in the awkward silence that followed Stick's comment. "We need more coffee," she announced. "People just keep coming." She glanced at the glass coffeemaker. Empty. An empty bag lay on the countertop. She opened the cupboard door. "Amy, where's the coffee?"

Amy got up and searched. "There isn't any."

"I'll get some," Ruthie offered.

"No, you won't!" Stick said, standing up. "I mean," he added quickly, "not alone. It's . . . it's raining hard out there."

Mrs. Ryan turned to stare up at his tall, lanky frame. "You're wet," she observed. "You didn't ride that bicycle of yours here in the rain, did you?"

"Oh no, ma'am. My mom dropped me off since she needed the car to get to work at eleven. I got wet taking the bike out of the trunk."

"And just how do you plan to ride that bike through all the flooding going on out there?" she asked.

"I'll go as far as I can," he said, "then I'll swim."

Mrs. Ryan's light laughter joined the others, but the gleam in her eyes was serious. "Take our car, Ruthie," she said, looking up at Stick. "And, Stick, you go along to protect her."

With my life, Mrs. Ryan, Stick thought. *With my life.* But of course he couldn't say that. "No problem, Mrs. Ryan."

He turned quickly, wondering if Ruthie would refuse to let him go with her. A few months ago she would have put ther hands on her hips, shook those red curls of hers, and said something like, "Stick Gordon couldn't protect a flea—let alone me!" And she'd refuse to get near him.

He let out a small sigh of relief when he heard only a small groan from her as she followed him out of the kitchen. As soon as they got outside, he held out his hand. "If you give me the keys, I'll drive."

When she did, he figured she was too upset to argue about it. On the way to the convenience store just a few blocks away, she filled him in on all she knew about Natalie and the escaped prisoner.

Stick told her that Andy Kelly, the youth group leader, had called him. "Grandpa prayed about it with me and Mom before we left," he shyly admitted as he pulled up as close as he could to the store. "Looks like we're the only brave souls around," he said, noting the empty parking lot.

When they had bought the coffee, he dared to ask about Sean. "Are you two getting back together?"

"That's over, Stick. I thought you knew that."

He shrugged and leaned forward to better see the road through the sheeting rain. "Well, you called him."

"No, I didn't. I called the Pizza Parlor to see if Natalie had been there. Phyllis is the one who handed the phone to him. That's why I talked to him. I do care about him as a person, Stick. You don't quit caring just because you break up. I mean, you've always been crazy about Amy—and you probably always will, no matter what."

Not as crazy as you think, Stick thought to himself. "But Sean's not selling drugs now, so he's . . . improving."

Ruthie huffed. "You don't have to try to protect me from the truth about Sean. Everyone knows what he's doing. And running a betting service on ball games isn't right. . . ." She began to tell him about the article she'd written. "It helped me put everything into perspective," she said.

They pulled up to the Ainsworths' house and parked at the sidewalk. "Why don't you put your bike in the trunk," Ruthie suggested. "We'll take you home." She opened her door just enough so that the dome light came on.

"That's okay," he said. "Why should I be dry when Natalie's out there somewhere in all this?"

Ruthie turned back to him. "Oh, Stick," she said softly, and her eyes clouded over.

He turned to reach up and brush away her tears. But he remembered his grandpa's warning, *"When in doubt about something, don't do it."* Instead, he had a better idea. "Close the door," Stick said gently.

Ruthie shut the car door, plunging them into near darkness.

Stick moved toward her, and Ruthie remembered the time when Sean had been so angry that he pushed her out of his car. Stick leaned over and grasped her hands, saying, "Could we . . . pray about them?"

Ruthie nodded. Over the phone, Sean had said he hoped Natalie would be all right. But she knew that hope didn't change much. Prayer did!

Her scalding tears turned to comforting warm ones as they bathed her cheeks. Stick's words didn't flow easily, but effort meant the world to Ruthie as he said a heartfelt prayer for her best friend, Natalie—and her former boyfriend, Sean.

＝＝＞

The silence was heavy when Frank didn't answer immediately about whether or not he intended to take Natalie with them. Then Henry spoke up. "Leave me if you want to, Frank. But if you leave Natalie, you'll be responsible for whatever happens to this girl."

"At this moment, I don't know what to believe about you or the girl, and I'm tempted to leave you both here. But I have a sister to help. Where's your jacket, Val?"

"On the couch," she said.

When he released her to grab the jacket, she made a mad dash toward the door and Frank had to run after her. He caught her again and kept a tight grip on her arm. He opened the front door, letting in a blast of wind and rain. Val put up her hand protectively. "I don't want to go. Let me go back to bed."

"You can't, Val. There's no power, and the phones are out. You're in no condition to be here alone. And if this valley floods like it's threatening to do, you'll be stranded here for weeks. Have you stocked up on food?"

Val tried to shrug away from him, and they all knew she hadn't.

"You may need my help, Frank," Henry said.

"I don't care if you stay here and drown!" Frank blared.

Val stopped struggling. "I'll go if you let Henry go." She slipped into her jacket, then grabbed hold of Henry's arm.

After a huge sigh, Frank took her other arm and went out through the front doorway.

Natalie wondered if that meant she could go, too. She closed the door behind herself and followed along.

They slogged across the sodden yard to the Bronco. She hoped Frank wouldn't make her take her mom's car. The Bronco was larger and higher off the ground, with bigger tires. It would surely do a better job on these muddy back roads.

Natalie sloshed ahead of them through deep puddles. She held open the back door of the Bronco. Her tennis shoes mired up in the soggy earth. Val and Henry climbed in back, then Natalie jumped into the front passenger seat.

"I feel sick," Val said.

"Here. Lie down." Henry helped her lie on the seat, and he knelt on the floorboard. They talked in hushed tones, but Natalie could hear some of it.

"Don't tell them, Henry," she was pleading. "I'm sorry. I didn't know what else to do."

"Your parents will help you," Henry was saying. "Frank will."

"No. They'll hate me. If they know, they'll hate me."

"No, Val. I didn't understand what the gambling habit could do. It's like alcoholism. A person has to have help."

"Excuses," Frank muttered and started the engine. Apparently he'd heard their conversation, too. When he turned the Bronco, Natalie was shocked at what the headlights revealed. Very little ground could be seen. But the road that slanted downward from the knoll appeared to be okay. If the bridge was intact, they'd soon be across it and going upward, toward the levee.

"Oh boy," Frank muttered. He squinted through the darkness. It had begun to rain hard again. Natalie strained to see ahead. The windshield wipers were *slop-slop-slop*ping across the windshield, but that didn't help the visibility. Then the Bronco stalled. Frank couldn't get it started. He opened his door and looked down. "It's flooded," he said.

Everyone was silent—waiting for whatever might happen next. Natalie remembered when she was learning to drive. She was with her dad. The car had stalled. He said it was flooded—too much gas. They'd have to wait. Is that what happened now? Slowly, her eyes searched the dark outline of Frank's face. She couldn't read his expression because he was like a dark shadow. "You mean . . . flooded with gas?"

Frank opened his mouth to inhale deeply. Then quietly, he replied, "No."

She knew then that water was over the bridge. It must be pretty deep.

She felt it first, the light swaying of the car. Then she heard it. A roar that reminded her of when the tornado hit Garden City.

Frank began frantically to turn the key in the ignition, grinding the starter, but the engine wouldn't turn over.

Henry got off his knees beside Val and leaned over the front seat. "We've got to get out of here, Frank. Get back up to the house."

Frank gulped. "I'm . . . not too good in water."

Val sat up groggily, then wild-eyed, looked out and saw the headlights shining on a sea of rushing water and felt the car rocking. She began to scream and grabbed hold of Henry. "What's happening?"

"Either the river has risen above flood stage, or part of the levee has given way. We've got to get to higher ground."

"I can't go out in that."

"You can't stay here."

"Yes I can." She sat up and swung her legs off the seat. Then she screamed again and lifted her feet. Her house slippers came off. "L-look!"

They didn't need to look. They already knew water was seeping onto the floorboard of the car.

"We've got to get out while we can," Henry said. "If we don't, we won't be able to open the doors and we'll be swept away. There's a big apple tree up ahead. If we can make it to that, we'll be okay."

"I can swim," Natalie said.

"Swim?" Val shrieked. "It's not that deep. We'll walk. We'll do as Frank said and go back to the house. We should have stayed there in the first place, like I wanted to do."

"Frank," Henry said in a too-calm voice that sounded ominous, "there's no way we can get up to the house. The bridge is gone."

"Yeah, I know," Frank replied. "Let's go for the tree."

Henry began to instruct them. "When we open the doors, the water's going to rush in. We have to be ready to jump out. The car could even turn over. Val, stay close to me. Frank, get over on the passenger side with Natalie. I'll count to three and say go. One. Two. Three. Go!"

Henry and Natalie opened the doors, struggling against the force of the rushing water. They jumped out, Frank right behind Natalie, and Val hanging on to Henry. "C-cold," Val said, echoing the feelings of the others as the water soaked through their shoes and pants. They linked arms and found their balance, picking their feet up out of the water, walking against the current of it, feeling themselves being pushed back. The water was up to their shins.

"You might try calling for help," Natalie said to Henry.

"There's nobody to hear," he said.

"My phone."

"I forgot," Henry said. He ripped open the Velcro on his jacket and brought out the cell phone. Just then a big piece of debris struck his legs. He lost his balance in the water, now knee-deep, and the phone went flying. It sank into the water and disappeared.

The current was moving too fast to consider trying to retrieve the phone. There seemed only one hope left—Henry's gun. Natalie didn't think Henry would need to shoot any of them now. The water was the big force to be reckoned with. "Maybe if you fired your gun," she suggested, "someone would hear."

"Gun?" Frank and Val both questioned. They stood rooted as if the water couldn't move them at that moment.

Henry reached into his pocket and drew out his hand, palm up. On it was a stick. "My gun," he said disgustedly.

He turned his hand, and Natalie watched the stick hit the water and move harmlessly away. A stick! That's what she'd feared from the time he jumped into the car. That he might shoot her. Now that feared object was nothing but a harmless piece of wood. What she had now hoped was a gun, which might bring someone to rescue them, was no help at all—a huge, cruel joke.

Quickly, she turned to head in the direction of the apple tree. Suddenly, she sank into thigh-deep water. Frank lost his grip on her arm, almost losing his balance. Val slipped, too, and began to scream while Henry held on to her and finally got stabilized.

Natalie was able to stand, but she was sopping wet and shivered uncontrollably from the cold. So did the others. She could actually hear their teeth chattering.

"Let me go first," Henry said. "Then we can hang on to each other's jackets and move forward in a line. That must be the ditch that runs along the edge of the trees. We're getting closer."

In single file, they were able to trudge again through the ever deepening water. Then the shadowy silhouettes of trees came into view.

The water was rising fast, but at least it was pushing them toward the trees instead of away. By the time they took a couple more steps, the water was waist-deep.

Henry reached a tree. "Climb up as high as you can on a good-sized branch," he instructed. "Natalie, you go first, and you can help pull Val up."

The gnarled old apple tree wasn't hard to climb. The water was halfway up the short trunk that was divided where several large limbs branched off. Natalie was able to reach for a branch, put one foot in the center of the trunk, and swing up onto a big limb that had several others close enough that she felt safe reaching down for Val. At the same time, Henry was trying to push Val into imitating what Natalie had done.

Natalie caught hold of Val's arm. "Just look up at the branches," she encouraged. Val came up, then settled back against the trunk, holding on to two branches on either side of her. Natalie positioned herself on one of the larger limbs, near Val. Henry hoisted himself up.

Frank followed easily.

Luckily, Natalie thought, this was the kind of tree made for climbing. The four of them each had a safe seat, although Frank was still trying to get situated on his. They could lean back against the largest part of the tree, sit on a good-sized branch, and brace themselves on other branches. It was sort of like being cradled, she tried to tell herself, rather than thinking of the water below, still rising ever higher. When would the water reach their level? Natalie looked up and saw only darkness. She longed for the moon or a star or some sign that God knew the situation they were in and would do something about it—soon.

Just then, Frank shifted his weight, apparently trying to situate himself more comfortably. He reached up for a smaller branch. It broke. He grappled for a handhold but slipped and fell into the water.

Val began to scream. His head came up and terrified, strangled sounds came from his throat. He was thrashing about in the water, trying to stand, but the water was too deep and the current was sweeping him away.

Both Val and Henry called, "Frank! Frank!" No other sound was heard in the dark night but rushing water and falling rain. Frank was nowhere in sight. The only place their eyes could see was where the car's headlights still shone out across the churning water.

Then Frank appeared in the headlights. He was trying to get to the Ainsworth car to have something to hold on to. But the water was splashing up over the lights. Then the lights wavered and grew fainter as the car turned and was swept away by the current. Again, Frank disappeared.

Quickly, Henry moved along the limb. "You two sit

tight. You'll be okay. I'm going after Frank."

"You'll drown, Henry. Stay here," Val pleaded. "I'm scared."

Natalie saw Henry hesitate for a moment. Maybe he was waiting for her to beg him to stay. She prayed silently, *Dear God, help Henry make the right decision.* It was all she could think. This was completely out of her hands. She'd thought she'd given her life over to God, but she'd never really been in an out-of-control situation like this. There was nothing else to hang on to. A tree limb certainly wasn't enough. It hadn't been enough for Frank.

"I have to go after him, Val. I'm sorry," he said, and the last words they heard after he slipped down into the water were, "I love you, Val." Then, distantly, his fearful voice was calling, "Frank! Frank!"

No answer came.

Then Henry stopped calling.

The only sound in the pitch-black night was the sporadic splashing against the tree as the water kept rising.

Ten

Jim Ainsworth jumped every time the phone rang. He kept thinking it was the prison calling to say they had news. But it wasn't the prison. People were calling to say they were praying. The police to say they'd found neither the car nor Natalie. Dr. Stiles to say that Natalie had not been taken to any area hospital. Others called, offering to help. He appreciated their thoughtfulness but felt so helpless. Natalie was his daughter, for whom he was responsible, and he could do nothing but sit and wait.

He felt a hand on his shoulder and looked up to see his wife's sympathetic face. "Why don't you go back to the prison, honey?" Jill suggested. "Then you'll be right there if any information comes in. We'll be all right. We have a lot of loving people around us here." She tried to smile, but her lips trembled.

"You're sure?" he asked.

Jill nodded and he hugged her close, then grabbed his jacket and headed for the door just as she said, "Be careful."

He turned to look at his wife. Jill had told him earlier that those were the last words she'd said to Natalie.

"I will," he said, giving her a kiss. "And don't worry . . . I *will* find Natalie."

As soon as Jim reached the prison, he went directly

to the office of the associate warden, Dick Grumley. Lieutenant Landry was still there, and so was Carl Sisk. They'd long been off duty but were determined to stay and find out what they could about the prisoner and Jim's daughter.

Warden Grumley told Jim what he knew. "All the law-enforcement agencies in any of the areas where Miller might go have been contacted. Missouri police are watching the Richardsons' house in Cape Girardeau, just in case Miller goes there—and the Kentucky state patrol is staking out his mother's home in Paducah. Of course, we expect him to be trying to get to his wife. They live in the old Richardson home down in the area across the river from Cape Girardeau. That area was evacuated this afternoon and was reported clear by four o'clock. Now, unless Miller's wife returned to that house, no one's there."

"Except Miller and my daughter!" Jim stormed, running his fingers through his hair. A deep pain surged through his head, and he closed his eyes. "We've got to get to them."

"All the roads to that area are closed."

"What difference does that make to a desperate convict?" Jim blared, and they all knew he had a point. An escaped prisoner didn't turn back when the going got tough—instead, he became like a caged animal, who didn't operate on good sense but on the instinct for survival.

The phone rang, and Grumley picked up. "No!" he said, closing his eyes tightly and leaning back against his chair. "Can't you do something? Miller may have the girl out there!"

"What is it?" Jim demanded to know.

"The Cape Girardeau police can't get down to the farmhouse," he said. "The Mississippi floodgates were opened about thirty minutes ago to relieve the pressure of the river on the levee."

Jim stared at Grumley, who didn't meet his eyes. "I've got to do something," Jim said, feeling more desperate than he had in his entire life.

"I'm right with you, Jim," Landry said, coming over to him, "until all this is settled. I'll do whatever you say."

Carl Sisk stood. "Me too, Jim, if you'll let me. I feel responsible."

Jim shook his head. He didn't blame Carl. "You did your job the way any of us would. We all know how easy it is for a minimum security prisoner to walk away if he decides to."

"Yeah," Carl agreed. "But he walked away from me! I'm going after him. But finding your daughter is first priority. Mind if I come with you?"

Jim walked over and clasped Carl's arm. "I'd welcome it, Carl," he said.

"Then I'll stay here and make personal calls for you, Jim," Landry offered.

"Thanks," Jim said, knowing Grumley would be busy with official business.

"But remember, Jim," Grumley reminded him. "We don't know for sure that Natalie and Miller are together."

Jim felt like he *did* know. But there was the slim possibility that Natalie's disappearance had nothing to do with Miller. "I'm going to drive up and down every street in Garden City until I'm sure there's been no accident and Natalie isn't stranded out there somewhere."

"Let's go," Carl said, more than ready.

Just as they started out the door, the phone rang again. Jim waited. Grumley hated to tell him this, more than the previous message. "It's too late, Jim. They can't close the gates, and the area at the Richardson farmhouse is now flooded. If they're out there, they could be safe at that house. It's high on a knoll."

"I've got to get out there," Jim said.

"You can't, Jim. There's no way in for several days except by helicopter. And then, only if the storm abates and visibility improves."

"I've got to know if my daughter and that convict are alone together at that farmhouse," Jim said.

Grumley nodded. He tried calling the farmhouse, got no answer, and contacted the phone company, who informed him the lines were down in that area. He looked on the file sheet at the list of people allowed to visit Henry Miller. "I'll contact the Richardsons and Henry Miller's mother. They already know that Miller has escaped, but maybe he's contacted them. They might be able to tell us something."

He made the call to Henry's mother. No one answered the phone. "That area is low-lying," Grumley said. "It was probably evacuated."

He punched in the phone number of Fred Richardson, who picked up on the first ring. After Grumley identified himself and explained the reason for his call, Mr. Richardson began to shout angrily. Grumley pushed the intercom button so Jim could hear the conversation. Mr. Richardson was obviously upset at being contacted by the prison and fearful because he hadn't heard from his son and daughter. He'd been waiting for a call.

Jim listened intently as Fred Richardson expressed his concern about his own daughter. "My wife, Virginia, called Val to ask her to come to our house after work since the weather's so bad. But Val said she was stopping by to see her brother, Frank. Later on, we called to make sure she was okay. Frank said she hadn't shown up. He called the farmhouse and got no answer, so he said he'd go out and check on her. That's the last we heard, and Virginia's frantic to hear something."

Fred Richardson sounded scared, much like Jim

felt. Richardson's daughter had apparently been a victim of Henry Miller . . . and now, Natalie.

"Mr. Richardson," Grumley was saying, trying to get a word in edgewise. "Has anything happened that could indicate Henry might be at the farmhouse? Have you received any hang-up calls or noticed anything suspicious?"

"Frankly, yes!" the man blurted. "Henry has written and called, begging us to talk to him. Well, we have nothing to say, and he has nothing to tell us that we want to hear." He hesitated a moment. "Val has seemed more troubled lately. Maybe she knew he was up to something, or he could have threatened her. I tell you one thing. If Henry Miller is out at the farmhouse, that only means trouble. That boy is bad news."

"Mr. Richardson, if you hear anything at all, about any of them, we need to know. I hate to say this, but we think Henry stole a car and took a young girl with him." Grumley gave a description of Natalie.

"Unbelievable!" Fred Richardson mumbled, then corrected himself. "No, not really unbelievable. He ruined my daughter's life. I wouldn't put anything past him."

"Have you called your son recently?"

"I keep trying but get no answer."

"Do you suppose Henry could have shown up there?"

"Now, that's a real possibility," said Mr. Richardson. "Frank and Henry used to be good friends. Henry's tried to get us to talk to him, but we didn't have any more to do with him after his arrest. I've let it be known if he ever shows his face here again, it will be the last time. So I suppose he could have gone to see Frank. Maybe Val knew about it and that's why she said she had to see her brother. Virginia said she didn't sound well when she talked to her."

"We'll check it out," Grumley said. "And, Mr. Richardson, I understand the farmhouse is in a flood zone. Is that correct?"

"A lot of the land out there is a flood zone. If anyone's out on the roads leading to it right now, then they might be in trouble. But we never worry about floodwaters reaching the farmhouse itself. It's been standing for decades—my parents built it. Val and Frank and Henry know the low roads and the high roads, so I don't think that's a concern. At least, not unless they open the floodgates."

That remark was one none of them wanted to hear!

Grumley didn't mention to Mr. Richardson that the floodgates had already been opened. "We'd appreciate your letting us know if you find out anything at all." He gave his number.

"Yes, sir. I'll do that."

After they ended the conversation, Jim asked, "Now what?"

Grumley looked grim. "We make calls and we wait."

About thirty minutes later, the police reported that no one was home at Frank Richardson's apartment and his car was gone. Jim surmised then that Frank had indeed gone to the farmhouse.

Jim visualized the possibilities. They could be stranded in a car or washed downstream. They'd have to check all the rescue operations. All the evacuation centers—schools—wherever people from the flooded areas were staying. Then he'd check with Dr. Stiles again. He could get information about hospitals in areas other than around here.

⌐———⌐

Val expressed what Natalie tried not to think as she said, in a trembling voice and through chattering teeth, "They . . . they . . . Frank and Henry are gone. Out in the dark, with nothing to hold on to. The Bronco's gone. We . . . we're going to die."

That thought had been in Natalie's mind ever since Henry had jumped into the car back at the college. Now it seemed even more likely that she wasn't going to survive this night. She didn't want to say it out loud, but she knew from living in the area that floodwaters didn't simply come up and disappear. Sometimes they kept rising—long after the rain had stopped.

And yet, would God let her be in this situation if there were not a good reason? He knew she was here. He had a reason for this tree to be in this very spot, where they had been able to seek refuge, at least for a time. The words of a song she'd sung in church entered her mind. The song spoke about the raging tempest and a person determined to be like a tree, planted by the waters. She especially remembered the words "I shall not be moved." It meant that one's faith in God should not waver—no matter what.

Is my faith that strong, Lord? I really don't want to die— not yet. I want to see my family. I want to see Scott. I want to get married and have children. I want a career. A career? She'd never decided what to do with her life. She'd asked God. She wanted His will done in her life. But He'd never revealed anything specific. At least . . . not yet.

Maybe . . . the reason was . . . that she wasn't going to have a career. Maybe her life was near an end. Maybe she didn't have a future in this world! Her parents had always told her how important it was to live each day as if it were your last. She had never seriously thought that she could die young. That only happened to other people.

How long did she have? How long before the creeping water made them climb higher and higher until they could go no farther? Would the tree roots hold, or would the tree be uprooted any minute, tossing them into the water? How long did it take to drown? How long could she hold her breath, grapple around in the water? Would she try to save Val . . . or only herself?

Oh, God. Help me do the right thing. I shall not be . . . I shall not be moved.

Natalie suddenly noticed Valerie clinging to the branch below her. She was crying softly and shaking uncontrollably, obviously terrified at what lay before them. *What about Valerie, Lord? Does she even know you? I know that Jesus is with me, but what about her? Should I say something, Lord? And if so, what?*

Natalie felt a new strength come into her as she clung to her branch. *"Tell her the truth!"* The words seemed almost as if they had been spoken aloud. Of course! At a time like this, what else mattered? Only the truth! Jesus said, "I am the way, the truth, and the life."

"Val," Natalie began with a calmness she could hardly believe, "are you a Christian?"

Val didn't answer for a minute, but then Natalie heard her quiet voice. "Yeah . . . I guess. I believe in God."

Natalie thought of the verse in the Bible that said the devil believes in God, but that didn't make him a Christian.

"Being a Christian is believing Jesus is the Son of God and that He gave His life for us, Val. It means giving our lives to Him and living for Him."

Val sighed. "I've been to church, and I've heard all that. I believed it when I was a child. I guess I still do. But it hasn't been a part of my life. God . . . couldn't love me now. Not with the way I am and what I was planning to do."

"God loves you just the way you are, Val. And He can forgive anything if a person wants to change."

"Oh, you don't know. You've probably never done

anything wrong. You don't know what it's like to mess up your life."

"Henry said his mom and your parents would help."

"No they wouldn't . . . not if they knew the whole story. Do you think my parents and my in-laws would forgive me if they knew I was going to abort their grandchild?"

Natalie thought carefully before answering. "I can't speak for them, Val. But I know *God* will forgive you. And that's all that really matters."

"Oh no," Val suddenly wailed, "the water's up to my branch! Can we climb higher? It . . . it's coming up quickly."

Natalie's eyes strained to see what was around them. The rain had slackened some. A few black treetops rose out of the murky water like shadowy, groping arms. "Can you tell which direction the water's flowing?"

"It seems to be moving to my left," Val said, paying attention to the flow of the water around her bare feet.

Natalie didn't like what she had to ask Val, but with the water creeping up this tree, there was no alternative. "Can you swim over to that bigger tree to our left?"

"I'm so scared," Val replied, reflecting Natalie's own thoughts. "But I'll try. Can you . . . stay close to me?"

"I'll do my best," Natalie replied, wondering if she could be half this brave without someone else to distract her. However, there was no way to ignore that they were in the midst of the overflowing Mississippi River, with only a few treetops visible in a vast sea of water that continued to rise.

Natalie tried to remember life-saving courses she'd had, but the exercises had been done in a controlled environment with instructors ready to take over if anything went wrong. No such conditions existed here! This was the ultimate test of everything that was in her. And it would be easier to stay in this apple tree and let the water rise over her than let go of that limb and take chances in that cold, dark water. But her survival instinct was strong. She wanted to live. She wanted to be reunited with her family and friends. And she wanted Val to get her life straightened out.

"You sit up, and I'll come down to your branch," Natalie said, although she was afraid the limb could break with the weight of them both.

Val sat up, and Natalie carefully climbed down. She talked Val through every move as they lowered themselves into the water, still holding on to the tree limb. Natalie felt so cold the water actually seemed to warm her a little. "Now, together, don't think about anything but swimming to that tree straight ahead."

Natalie did not heed her own advice. Her whole life and everyone who'd ever meant anything to her were in her thoughts and in her heart. *Cissy? What was her good news? And Katlyn?*

If I don't get out of this, Katlyn will have a clear road to Scott—and she's wanted him as far back as I can remember. Scott! Will I ever see him again?

Eleven

Scott Lambert couldn't believe what he was hearing when Cissy called to say Natalie was missing. Everything that Natalie meant to him was flashing through his mind as Cissy explained how she might have been abducted by an escaped prisoner and was possibly caught in the flood.

"Say this is some kind of cruel joke, Cissy," Scott said incredulously. Surely this wasn't true. But his cousin's frantic voice confirmed the truth of it. It even sounded likely, with the prison being right outside Garden City, with Natalie having driven her mom to the college, and the prisoner himself having been at the college.

But Scott didn't want to believe that. Even after Cissy said she had to get off the phone and would call him when any news at all turned up, he stared at the snow dome Natalie had given him for Christmas. It matched the snow dome he had given her. Each had a different scene of New York, but both included the Empire State Building.

He picked up the dome and turned it upside down, then righted it and watched the snow fall. *I'll never forget you,*" he'd told her when the two of them stood at the top of the Empire State Building in New York last Thanksgiving holiday. Cold snow had fallen all around them, but she had warmed him with her sweet kiss. He'd told her he would never forget her and made her promise to meet him in that very spot after she graduated from college.

He'd put their relationship on hold—expecting her to wait for him for four years. What was he thinking? Now, guiltily, he realized he didn't think of Natalie as often as he should. She was finishing her senior year in high school, while he was getting on with his career in photography and modeling. It was easy to get caught up in being in the spotlight and having beautiful girls give the impression he was pretty special.

But it was Natalie who was special—not for the way she looked, or styled her hair, or what she wore. What mattered most to her was her faith in God.

He and Natalie had survived a tornado together, then had worked on projects to help those who had experienced great losses in the storm. It was Natalie who encouraged him when he was so troubled about his mom's alcoholism. It was Natalie who had stood by him when his brother, Zac, got drunk and had that awful accident that injured Katlyn.

I should have stayed in Garden City and finished out my senior year with Natalie. Without her, I'm not as close to God. I've thought a lot more about my career than I have of her and what's important to her. And instead of influencing Antonio Carlo for the Lord, Antonio was influencing him. Not that Scott was doing anything so wrong, but he wasn't doing anything so right, either.

"I've got to go to Garden City," he explained to the Carlo family, in whose home he was staying while in New York.

Antonio and his parents agreed. But when Scott called the airlines, he discovered that all the airports near Garden City were closed due to high winds and flooding. He was determined to get there, but he wasn't sure how.

Where would I be without Natalie? he wondered. But he knew. He'd be lost. Maybe he'd have gone the way Zac chose—trying to drown his troubles with alcohol. Nat had been his lifeline. What could he do for *her*?

Right now he could start praying. He felt so helpless. She was far more important than the modeling jobs. He picked up a magazine that featured him on the cover. What good did it do to have your picture plastered on magazine covers when your heart was so heavy? That's something Cissy had learned. He was now learning it, too. Maybe he should have turned down the modeling contracts. He needed to see Natalie—to tell her how much good she'd done in his life.

Please, God, don't let any harm come to her. She's the best person I've ever known. And I need to tell her . . . that I love her.

The Carlos were willing to have Scott fly to Illinois in their company jet. But the same restrictions applied as with commercial flights. No planes could land anywhere near Garden City. The weather was just too bad.

Scott kept trying to call. He knew he was being a nuisance, but he had to know if they'd heard anything about Natalie.

Every time he called the Ainsworths' number, he got a busy signal.

He called home. His parents didn't answer.

He called Cissy's parents. No answer.

He called his aunt Martha and discovered that his parents, Cissy's parents, and several friends had gathered there to pray for Natalie. That was some relief, but scary, too. They apparently thought the worst.

Finally, he got through to the Ainsworth home. Amy answered and told him that they didn't know anything yet. Her dad was at the prison, the youth group was meeting and praying, their pastor had called a group in and he was at their house. So were Cissy and the Ryan family.

Ruthie Ryan—Natalie's best friend. She was always direct in what she had to say. "Could I speak with Ruthie, please?" he asked.

"Scott?" Ruthie said. "Oh, Scott. This is awful. We don't know, but we think the prisoner took Natalie and her mom's car. Mr. A said he didn't think the inmate was dangerous, but if he's got her, they may be in the middle of a flood. Everybody's praying."

"Yeah, I haven't stopped," he said.

"I think we all took Natalie for granted, Scott. Everybody's talking about what a difference she's made in all our lives. She thinks she's so ordinary, but she's not."

"I know that," Scott said, feeling the warm tears trickle down his cheeks. "She's unlike anyone I've ever known. I can't imagine this world . . . without her."

"I know," Ruthie said. "She's been such a good friend. When I broke up with Sean and thought I couldn't make it, Natalie helped me so much. I can't stand to think of anything bad happening to her."

Scott agreed. "I don't want to lose her, Ruthie."

⟶

Natalie was trying to wait for Val, a poor swimmer and nearly frightened out of her wits. Her every breath was a fearful gasp, and she fought the water instead of working with it. Fortunately, the current helped push them along without sweeping them under or away, and they managed to reach the huge oak. Getting into it proved easier, with their weight being supported by the water, than climbing into the apple tree had been. But as they pulled themselves out of the water, the weight of their wet clothing hampered their climb to the higher branches.

With Natalie's help, Val struggled to reach a limb several feet above the water. Natalie flung herself onto a nearby branch, close enough for them to touch each other. "Do you know how h-high we must be?" Val gasped.

"Don't think about it," Natalie cautioned, trying to remind herself it didn't matter. But what did concern her was how long the tree could stand in the water-logged ground. Could the roots hold?

Then Val took in a tortured breath and exhaled on a scream. "Oh no . . . no!"

"What?" Natalie said quickly.

"My stomach. It's cramping. Oh no. Please don't let me lose the baby here. Not . . . here."

What do I do? Natalie was near panic now. It would be bad enough to have to help with a miscarriage in the comfort of a home. What would she do if Val had a miscarriage while in a tree? Oh, this was unreal!

Or . . . too real!

A real nightmare! *Oh, God*, she prayed, not even knowing what to pray for. This was incredible. If ever she needed God, it was now. Never had she been so totally helpless. If there was to be any help, it would come only from God. And if ever they needed a miracle, it was now.

But no miracle came.

"I can't lose this baby here. Not in a tree. Not in a flood. Oh, God, help me," Val moaned. She laid her head against the big limb. "Maybe I should just slip off. Maybe . . ."

"No, Val!" Natalie knew she had to help Val—encourage her to hang on. Despite her own fears, Natalie could plainly see that Val was even more fearful. Maybe God wanted her here for Val's sake. She couldn't let her just give up. "We're here for a reason, Val. God wouldn't have let this happen if He didn't have a reason for it. We can either give up, or we can hang on and know God will help us. And, Val, you just asked for His help. He's here. Don't give up."

"Why is He doing this? Why?" Val cried.

Natalie didn't understand it all herself. "I don't know. But I know God is with us. I was in a tornado once . . . and then I was in a car wreck with a drunk driver. I don't know why these things happened to me, but I know that each time God was with me . . . and helped me."

As Natalie reassured Val of God's faithfulness, she felt her own strength being renewed. She was no longer concerned with whether or not she was going to die. She was here for Val . . . and she could focus on that.

In the midst of her human feelings of panic, worry, and fear, she felt a calmness, as if her eyes were opened in this darkness. If these were her last moments, what better way to spend them than to tell another person how she could be certain that this life was not the end . . . but a wonderful new beginning!

Henry didn't know if he'd made the right decision by going after Frank, but he had to try to save him. With Val and Natalie in the tree, he knew they were safe for now. At least they had a chance of surviving.

Oh, God, he kept praying. *I only wanted to make things right, but all I've done is make a worse mess. Please don't let all these people die because of me. Please help us!*

"Frank! Frank!" he kept calling.

Then, suddenly, Henry felt himself being pulled around, swirling, helpless to swim out of the undertow. If this was some kind of sewer system or a culvert, he knew he'd be pulled under with no chance of survival.

He'd lost all sense of direction, having no choice but to be carried along by the current.

He feared that Frank was already gone. How could Frank survive this? He couldn't even swim! As a bank president's son, Frank had grown up with calm swimming pools to play in, while Henry had been thrown in creeks, rivers, and lakes by laughing older kids ever since he was a young boy. He'd learned the hard way. But in later years it had paid off. He wasn't afraid of water, and whenever the floods had come, he'd always pitched in to help. But having seen the damage that raging floodwaters could do—and the lives lost—he held a great respect for water.

Maybe that's why he'd instinctively gone after Frank, having volunteered in years past to go into flooded areas. He'd grown up around this. Frank's experiences had been on higher, safer ground in Cape Girardeau.

Am I doing this to help Frank? he wondered. *Or am I really trying to help myself in some selfish way? To do something right for a change.*

I don't know if it's possible for me to do anything right anymore. I've gone too far. Even if I survive this, my life is over. Maybe it's best if I don't survive. What have I got to look forward to now? A lifetime in prison? Maybe if I just open my mouth and go under, it might be the best thing for everybody. I'm so tired. . . .

A sound caught his attention—maybe branches scraping against each other in this eddy he'd been drawn into. Eddy? Yes! That was it. This wasn't some kind of pipe to suck him under. It was swirling water, moving opposite the main current, and it would eventually calm.

"Frank! Frank!" he called frantically, now letting the water take him where it would instead of fighting it. He was being swung in a wide circle. If he could just keep breathing, relax as much as possible and go with the flow, he'd be all right.

Then he felt something. A cold, wet hand came across his face, and at the same time something hit him in the head. A person! "Frank?" he yelled and felt the hand on his shoulder, trying to grasp him, causing him to lose control. He went under.

With some difficulty, Henry got free from the flailing legs and thrashing arms and came up some distance away. "Grab the branch, not me!" he shouted.

The response from the other person was a choking sound, trying to clear the lungs of water. Henry knew they both would be carried around and around in circles, remaining distant from each other, unless he could swim against the flow. That would be almost impossible, for the force was great, and all sorts of debris were caught up in the eddy. But he had to try.

With all his might, Henry swam against the current, caught hold of huge limbs, and even felt something beneath his feet at one point that he thought could be a car. Maybe the Bronco! Then the huge limb with several branches was on him. He caught hold. "Frank? Is that you?"

The answer was a strangled sound. If it wasn't Frank, it was someone. He'd have to help whoever it was, if possible. He felt a small amount of comfort knowing someone else was there in that vast ocean of frigid water. Thinking of it, he realized he was cold clear through. Cold enough for hypothermia to set in.

"It's . . . me," Frank finally managed to choke out.

"Just hang on, Frank. We'll work our way out of here real soon."

"I'm stuck," Frank said breathlessly.

Henry grabbed on to a limb that was sticking out of the water. It was clearly the same limb Frank was stuck in.

"Let's just go with the flow, Frank. Try to rest against the limb."

"No choice," Frank rasped. "I think my right arm is broken. I can't feel it, and I can't seem to move it. Maybe it's just numb from being stuck in the branches."

Then suddenly Frank let out a yell. "My foot! It's caught now, too. I can't get it loose." He moaned pitifully and his head fell over onto the limb as if he'd passed out. The branch was swaying from side to side, trying to go with the current. Apparently, whatever was holding Frank's foot was keeping the tree limb from moving. Something would have to give—either the limb, whatever was holding it back, or Frank's foot!

Bone weary and cold, Henry didn't relish diving under the big limb to find out what was holding Frank back. He could easily get caught in the underwater debris. He considered the alternative. He could grab hold of another floating object and let it carry him downstream to safety.

Safety? What was he thinking? There was no safe place for him anymore. If he got out of this, he was facing a lifetime of prison and regrets. He had nothing to gain by moving toward so-called safety.

With difficulty, he forced himself under the branches of the big limb and came up beside Frank, whose breath was coming in short gasps. Henry took a deep breath and went under, feeling his way down Frank's body to his feet. Wrong foot!

He had to come back up for air and try again. This time he found the foot. It was wedged against a piece of metal. After a couple more tries, Henry had the distinct impression the foot was caught between the fender and tire of a vehicle. The foot was turned at an unnatural angle. Without caution, he yanked the foot out of the shoe and felt Frank slip away from him.

Coming up, gasping for air, he saw the silhouette of Frank against the limb, moving away from him. He mustn't let it out of his sight. He swam with all his strength, definitely limited now, against the current toward the limb. Just as he was about to reach Frank, something struck him in the ribs on the left side of his chest, causing excruciating pain and knocking the breath out of him.

For a long, agonizing moment, Henry was wedged between the limb Frank was on and what looked like a fence post. An attempt to take in a deep breath almost rendered him unconscious. He resorted to taking shallow breaths but felt the weight of the post crushing his ribs.

He couldn't climb onto Frank's limb, nor move to the side, or even go under the water. He was stuck. Just when he thought he could hold on to consciousness no longer, the opposite end of the post turned, gave a push at Frank's limb, then floated off with the current into the distance as if it were a harmless stick bobbing on a gently flowing stream. But serious damage had been done. Henry knew he was badly hurt.

Operating on sheer will, Henry wrapped his right arm around one of the branches and grasped a smaller branch attached to it. He laid the side of his head on the limb and forced himself to take in painful but precious breaths of air.

He could do no more. After a long time of simply trying to breathe and hold on, Henry realized Frank had made no sound at all. Was he sleeping? Unconscious? Henry felt so exhausted himself that he would welcome some respite, even if it meant slipping into the water and not bothering to fight his way to the top.

Then something flickered against his closed eyes.

He opened them, staring into the darkness, trying

to see farther than the few feet around him. A light was flashing ahead.

Was this the light he'd heard people see when they are about to die? But in his condition, it wouldn't be light he'd see upon his death, would it? He was sure heaven was not in his future.

Maybe in his exhaustion he was hallucinating. He laid his head against the limb again and closed his eyes. It didn't matter anymore. He was drifting off, and knew he might as well just drift . . . down. . . .

Twelve

"I don't know how you can be so calm, knowing we're going to die," Val said. "I'm shaking like a leaf."

Calm? Natalie thought about that. Throughout this ordeal she had felt jittery, faint, scared, uncertain, even panicked from one moment to the next. And yet there was an assurance that if she died, she'd go to be with God. There was the difference between the two of them—an assurance about eternity, or an uncertainty. Scott had talked about that. Scott's dad was a doctor, and he'd told Scott how different patients responded when death was certain. For a Christian, it was as if a welcoming angel was there to escort them from this life to an eternal home of peace and love. She knew that Val could experience that same assurance and peace, if she was willing to listen.

"I don't know what's going to happen to us, Val," Natalie said. "But I do know that I'm going to heaven when I die, and you can, too."

"How?" Val asked.

Natalie explained briefly how Val could give her life to God, thinking as she told her that it sounded too simple. "Just believe that Jesus is the Son of God and that He died for your sins. Ask His forgiveness and receive His Spirit into your heart." Natalie prayed aloud, and Valerie prayed after her.

After a long, silent moment, Val said, "I meant it, Natalie, but . . . I don't feel any different. I'm still scared."

"So am I, Val. But we're not alone."

"I don't *feel* forgiven. Whatever has happened to Henry and Frank is my fault. If they've died, it's my fault. What have I become?" she wailed. "I would kill my baby. And now I'm responsible for Frank and Henry. And even you. Why don't you just swim to safety, Natalie? After all I've done, I don't deserve to live."

Natalie knew she probably could swim to safety. The rain had stopped. The wind had calmed. She could see the shadowy outline of the farmhouse roof. Maybe she could swim to it. But would Val hang on if she left?

"I'm not leaving you, Val. God wants me here for a reason. Until He gets us out safely together, I'm staying."

"Even if God has forgiven me, Natalie, I can only bring pain and disappointment to my family. I've already done it to Henry. I want you to save yourself."

"Val," Natalie said. "You said you didn't feel any different after you asked Jesus to come into your heart. But I see a difference. Before, you were concerned only with yourself. That's changed. Now you're concerned about everyone else, even about me—a stranger."

"I don't know, Natalie," Val admitted. "If I feel differently, it's because I know we might never get out of this alive. My only hope right now is God—that He might hear me and help us. But if we come out of this, I'm going to face the same problems I've had all along—and even some new ones."

"But not alone, Val. God will help you. And He'll bring lots of people along to help you. I'm sure your family will help."

"I don't know, Natalie," Val said. "Look what I've done to them." She hugged the tree limb, and with the side of her face against it, she sobbed. "Natalie," she said finally, "will you do something for me? If I'm really turning all this over to God, I need a clear conscience. If you make it and I don't, will you tell my parents and Henry's parents what I'm going to tell you?"

"If you want me to."

"I do," Val said. "You talked about truth. I'm going to tell you the whole truth."

Natalie thought she knew the truth already. But through the dark, cold night, she listened to Valerie's words, her heartfelt confession, her truth. Natalie knew Valerie was really confessing to God, preparing her soul to meet her creator.

Valerie told Natalie all about the first time she'd ever gambled—the first time she'd ever gone to the Riverboat.

It was her sixteenth birthday, and Frank took her there as his present to her. Even now, hanging on to a limb in the top of a huge oak tree, Val could feel the urge, the excitement, almost as strong as the craving for survival from this flood.

That first time, however, had been like walking into an entirely new world. She'd dressed up and felt so grown-up. Frank had faked an ID for her and acted as if she were his girlfriend. She'd become one of a crowd of laughing, joking, happy people as wheels spun and bets were placed. She remembered winners shrieking with delight and losers trying again. There were glowing lights and background music—a world completely alien to anything she'd ever known.

"That world of gambling," Val said, "became my all-time fascination. At first it was just fun. It didn't matter if I won or lost. There was just something mesmerizing about playing the game."

Val spoke in a trembling voice so low she wasn't

sure Natalie could hear her. "Frank and I became much closer after that night. Before that, he was just my older brother, who looked out for me. But after that sixteenth birthday, he and I were more like equals."

"Does Frank have a problem with gambling?" Natalie asked.

Val was thoughtful for a moment. "No," she finally answered. "He can take it or leave it. We did go back to the Riverboat many times together, but while I spent my time gambling, he was more interested in being with his girlfriend than with me. When a guy would ask me out on a date, I'd suggest the Riverboat. Sometimes I lost all my allowance. Other times, I doubled it. Finally, I took a summer job and a Christmas holiday job to make money for gambling."

"Your family didn't know?" Natalie asked.

"No, they were proud of me that I wanted a job. They thought that was admirable because I didn't *have* to work, and they'd already put aside money for my college tuition. Oh, this sounds so awful now, Natalie."

"It sounds like an addiction," Natalie said.

"I guess so," Val sighed. "It sort of blocked out everything else for me." She felt herself choke on the truth of her words. "It became doubly exciting when Henry noticed me," Val continued. "He asked me out after I'd just begun my first year of college. Although he was a friend of Frank's and my parents liked him, they said I would have to double-date with Frank since Henry was four years older than me. I had already been in love with him for a long time."

Val remembered something Henry had said in those early dating days when she'd again asked him to go to the Riverboat with her. " 'You come here an awful lot, don't you, Val?' Henry asked me. I replied that it was my recreation and I didn't go any more often than guys watched football. And didn't they even bet on games? I always had an answer for everything.

"After we were married, it all got worse. We really didn't have much money, but I kept sneaking out to go gambling. Henry tried so hard to stop me, but I just couldn't. Finally, I took our entire life savings—eight thousand dollars. I was going to double or triple it. But I lost it all in . . ." Her voice trailed off.

Natalie said, "I didn't hear you."

"I said," Val confessed, this time sobbing so hard she had to say one word at a time, "I . . . lost . . . eight . . . thousand . . . dollars . . . in . . . five . . . minutes."

Val wished Natalie would condemn her, be angry with her. After all, wasn't it Val's own fault that Natalie was here in this danger? It all went back to Val's gambling. It had put Henry in prison. It had brought this innocent girl here.

Val could see it all so clearly now. While facing death, she was facing her own life.

"Henry will never tell on me," Val said. "You have the best chance of surviving, Natalie. You can tell my parents what I've done and that Henry only meant to borrow that money from the bank so he could help me. He was going to pay it back. He is—or was—a Christian before my sins got in the way and corrupted him."

"Even Christians can sin, Val," Natalie said. "I'm sure by now Henry has asked God to forgive him, and God will."

"But I'm responsible for Henry's being in prison. If you get out of this, clear Henry's name. Tell my parents that I'm truly sorry and ask them to . . . not hate me."

"They won't, Val," Natalie assured. "Parents love their children no matter what. You would, too."

Val cried aloud then. "Please, Natalie. Only you can set the record straight."

Is this my purpose? Natalie wondered. *To set the record*

straight to surviving parents of drowning victims? Are these people all going to drown? Will I be left to tell the story?

Val suddenly called out, sounding frantic. "Natalie, the water's creeping up my legs."

Should I swim to that taller tree? Natalie questioned. *Val says she can't make it. God, what should I do?*

She decided she would not abandon Val. She would stay with her . . . to the end.

"I want to give you this little white dove pin," Natalie said and explained that it symbolized God's Spirit. "Think of that, Val. He will give you courage."

"I can't reach up," Val said.

"I can pin it on your sleeve," Natalie answered and slowly, making sure she was well braced, reached to unfasten the pin.

The moment her fingers touched it, something moved. She didn't know if it was the entire tree, or if something had struck the limb she was on, but she heard a cracking sound. Her hands grasped for a limb but found none.

Suddenly, there was no limb beneath her, and she was plunging into the water below. Automatically, she drew in her breath as she fell backward. Her head hit on something.

The last thing Natalie heard was Valerie screaming, "Natalie! Natalie!"

The sound became muffled as Natalie felt herself going under the water, unable to breathe, unable to see, and she was losing all feeling, unable to think or act or help herself.

Death was cold and dark and painful as water, not air, filled her lungs.

Thirteen

Around three A.M. the first bit of information that came into the prison was from John Stiles, after he had called the Ainsworth home. Warden Grumley took the call and patched it through to Jim Ainsworth, who was searching Garden City and the surrounding area with Carl Sisk.

"Jim," Dr. Stiles said after they got a clear connection. "About an hour ago, a Frank Richardson was picked up by a rescue boat and was admitted to the Mercy Hospital down in Tanis. The location indicates this could be the Frank Richardson in question. Sorry I couldn't get to you sooner, but they're in a dire emergency situation."

"I appreciate this," Jim said, knowing even this information came through only because Dr. Stiles had considerable influence in the area. But right now, his primary concern was his daughter. "Anything on Natalie?"

"I'm sorry, Jim. No. The flooding has reached into unexpected areas, and some of the people being brought in are unidentified. But there wasn't anyone matching the description of Natalie."

"Could somebody talk to this Frank Richardson? Maybe he knows something."

When Dr. Stiles cleared his throat, Jim knew he

wasn't going to like John's answer. "Jim, the Richardson man is unconscious. But I will relay whatever information we get, just as soon as possible. The Mercy Hospital administrator understands the immediacy of this, believe me."

"Thanks, I . . ." Jim began contritely. He could never have gotten even that information on his own, without it first going through proper law-enforcement channels.

"No need for thanks, Jim. You'd do the same for me. I just wish I could do more."

The next call to the prison came from law-enforcement officials. A Bronco, registered to Frank Richardson, had been washed up along a sand-bagged bank at the edge of the little town of Tanis.

It seemed no one was sleeping that night, but every citizen from the surrounding areas was out helping the stranded, shining battery-operated lights out across the water as a signal, gaining and documenting information, exchanging soggy clothes for dry ones, making calls to inform next of kin.

"Was anyone picked up along with Frank Richardson?" Warden Grumley asked the caller. The reply was that several people had been picked up during the night. The area near Tanis was flooded. Rescue operations had been under way there. Many who had no identification on them were hurt and unable to give their names.

"What about a Natalie Ainsworth? Or Henry Miller? Valerie Miller?" The person checked their records. No such names were listed. Frank Richardson's parents had been notified and were on their way to Mercy Hospital.

After the phone conversation, Grumley relayed the message to Jim and Carl, who were still riding the streets between Garden City, Garden Acres, and Logan Junior College. "Helicopter personnel dropped down to the Richardson farmhouse, Jim. The water has completely flooded about four feet of the first floor, but no one was in the house."

"The car?" Jim asked, frenzied, hoping that somehow Natalie was not caught in that flood. He tried not to think about the car being flooded. If it overturned and Henry Miller got out, that could very well mean that Natalie was trapped. No! He mustn't give up. Mustn't jump to conclusions. There was no positive proof that Henry Miller and Natalie were together. It seemed likely, but they didn't really know. He must remember that and not let go of his hope, his prayers.

Then, as if to dash what hope he had left, Grumley said, "There was no sign of a car, Jim."

"We're heading down to Tanis right now," Jim said. "If I can't talk to Richardson, maybe his parents can give me some information."

"Be careful," Grumley said. "I'll call Jill to let her know that you've gone to Mercy Hospital."

The drive wasn't easy or safe as Jim and Carl drove through the flooded areas. There were many detours, trees uprooted, power lines down. At about four-thirty A.M. they reached the hospital.

The Mercy Hospital personnel were expecting Jim Ainsworth, due to calls from Dr. Stiles and the hospital administrator. Jim was to be given their utmost cooperation, as much as possible in such an emergency situation.

A head nurse was waiting when Jim and Carl arrived in the emergency room, ready to lead him to Frank Richardson's room. "His parents are here," she said.

"My daughter?" Jim asked. "Is she here?"

The nurse listened sympathetically to his description of Natalie. "We've had a number of young girls brought in during the night," she said. "Several have been treated and released, but a few have been admitted. Most of them were caught off guard by the flood and were carrying no identification. Does your daughter have any particular identifying marks?"

Jim had to say there were none. Natalie had no birthmarks or outstanding features. Just his beautiful daughter, with deep blue eyes, light brown hair that shone golden in the sunlight, a face that glowed with kindness, a heart filled with love. But unusual physical marks, no . . .

"Her mother said she was wearing jeans and a beige down jacket, tennis shoes . . ." His voice trailed off seeing the head nurse's expression, which seemed to say that description could fit just about any teenager.

Suddenly, a thought struck him. "She usually wore a little pin. A white dove. Maybe—"

Just then an intern walked up. "Did you say Natalie?" he asked.

"Yes! Yes!" Jim replied. "Is she here?"

"There's a girl back there in cubicle six that keeps saying something that sounds like 'Natalie.' "

Jim didn't wait for permission but with determined steps strode toward the curtain.

The head nurse began to thumb through the pages of the clipboard she held. "Oh, Mr. Ainsworth," she protested, but he'd already pushed the curtain aside and stepped inside the cubicle.

Jim stopped short, seeing several attendants surrounding the bed where a pale young woman lay hooked up to IVs. Astonished, he stared disbelievingly at her short dark curls. He stepped backward, almost losing his balance, and grasped the curtain. He turned around, looking at the head nurse and at Carl standing beside her. His face fell, his sleepless eyes burned, and his words seemed to rake his throat when he declared helplessly, "That's not Natalie."

"I'm so sorry," the head nurse told Jim. She surveyed the report. "The woman in cubicle six was picked up in the area between Tanis and the levee."

"That would be the vicinity of the Miller farmhouse," Jim said to Carl. "Could that young woman be Henry Miller's wife?"

"There was no identification on her," the nurse said regretfully.

"Have the Richardsons seen her?" asked Carl.

"No," the nurse said. "They're with Frank Richardson on the third floor."

Jim looked over his shoulder at cubicle six, then back at the nurse and Carl. He said hopefully, "Then this girl could be the Richardsons' daughter."

Carl was nodding. "She might know something."

"When can we talk to her?" Jim asked.

"I'll speak with the doctor," the nurse said and headed for the back of the room. When she returned, she had little information. "She's in a state of shock. She is saying words that we will try to make sense of. Mainly, she's concerned about her baby. The doctors are afraid she might lose it."

Jim closed his eyes for an instant against the terrible thought. *Jill and I don't want to lose our baby, either. Our first baby girl. My Natalie.*

Fourteen

Jim and Carl went to the door of room 324. The patient in the bed with his head bandaged looked pale and was either sleeping or unconscious. One foot was on top of the sheets with a cast on it. His right arm, also in a cast, lay across his chest. A middle-aged woman sat in a chair looking at him, and a man stood staring out at the early gray morning. At least the rain had stopped.

Jim stepped inside. "Mr. and Mrs. Richardson?"

"Yes?" The woman in the chair spoke as the man at the window turned.

"I'm sorry to disturb you," Jim said, "but I was told the patient in this room might be able to tell me something about Henry Miller."

The man's glance swept over Jim's and Carl's uniforms. "He's unconscious," Mr. Richardson said. "But I can tell you plenty about Henry Miller! The police said he escaped. Are you conducting the investigation?"

"I'm an officer at the federal prison," Jim replied. "My name is Jim Ainsworth. This is my partner, Carl Sisk. We're trying to locate my daughter. As you have heard from Warden Grumley, we have reason to believe that Henry abducted her at Logan Junior College and got away in my wife's car."

Mrs. Richardson groaned. "I'm so shocked that Henry would do such a thing." She bit on her lip and looked longingly at her son in the hospital bed.

"We didn't think he'd do a lot of the things he's done," Fred Richardson ground out, obviously upset. He leaned back against the window ledge and grimaced. "We should never have allowed Valerie to marry that scum bucket."

"We still don't know if he or Frank went to the farmhouse," Mrs. Richardson said, her voice breaking. "We don't know if Val is safe." She threw away her used tissue and reached for another.

Jim knew how they felt—having a daughter who was missing in the worst flood to hit the area in decades.

"Is your daughter expecting a baby?" Jim asked.

"No," both Richardsons said at once, looking at him curiously.

"Why would you ask that?" Mr. Richardson said.

"There's an unidentified young woman in the emergency room who was brought in from the general area of the farmhouse that I thought . . . hoped . . . just might be her."

A groan sounded from the bed. They all stared. Frank was trying to open his eyes. "Val," he said.

The stunned group stared at him. Mr. Richardson rushed over to the side of the bed. "What about Val, Frank? Did you see her? Is she all right?"

At the same time, Jim asked, "Do you know anything about Natalie?"

"In a tree," he said and tried to focus on Jim. "Natalie . . . brave girl."

"So Miller did have her," Carl said as Jim made eye contact with him.

As Frank regained consciousness, he was able to give his account of the flood—as much as he could remember at that point. "Natalie was a very brave girl, Mr. Ainsworth," he said. "Henry did an unforgivable thing by taking her hostage, I know, but he wouldn't have intentionally hurt her."

Mr. Richardson began to pace the floor. "You're defending Henry? The guy who ruined your sister's life and has made ours a disaster?"

"No, I'm not defending what Henry did. But there are things he told me. About—" He stopped talking and closed his eyes and his mouth against whatever he was about to say.

"What, Frank?" his mother encouraged. "Are we tiring you too much?"

"No," Frank said. "We need to talk to Val."

Silence fell on the group. Jim knew what everyone was thinking. Where was Val? Where was Natalie? Would they be all right? Was this the last thing he was ever to hear about his daughter? Some stranger saying she was brave in the face of her kidnapper and a flood? *Oh, God*, he prayed, *be with Natalie in a special way, taking care of her needs in this time of trouble. Lord, you know I want to see my daughter again.*

"Henry saved my life." Frank's sudden declaration startled them.

They all looked at him.

"I know that doesn't excuse him," Frank went on. "But if my life is worth anything, then Henry's actions should count for something. Sure, we should blame him where that is due, but shouldn't we also credit him where that is due? Help me sit up," Frank said, trying to lift himself.

Mr. Richardson cranked up the top of the bed. Frank laid his head back on the pillow and closed his eyes. Slowly, like one awakening from a long sleep, he told more details as they came back to him—about the rushing water, the tree, Natalie and Val climbing to safety, the tree limb breaking, then Henry coming after him.

"Yes, Henry was wrong to take Natalie," he said so quietly the others had to strain to hear his words. "But he wouldn't have hurt her. He didn't know they'd get into a flood. He just wanted to get to Val."

"Did he get to Val?" Mr. Richardson demanded to know.

"Yes," Frank said, then other questions poured from his parents. "She . . . and Natalie . . . in a tree. Henry . . . saved my life." Each word was growing fainter now, and his head relaxed. His lips parted with deep breathing.

"Frank? Frank?" his mother said gently, but he didn't answer. She looked up at Jim. "The doctor said he would be drifting in and out of consciousness for a while. That's the most he's talked." She picked up his hand and held it between hers, saying expectantly, "A little color is coming back into his face."

"I don't know how he can say anything good about Henry Miller," Mr. Richardson blazed, looking at Jim. "Henry took all the joy from my daughter's life. He had every chance. I gave him a job at the bank. He embezzled. I gave him my daughter. He destroyed her emotionally." His face reddened and he lifted his hands as if to choke someone. "I just hope I get my hands on him." Mental anguish was evident in his bloodshot eyes and weary voice.

Jim understood. Frank had confirmed that Miller kidnapped Natalie. He was totally responsible for anything happening to her. Jim would do his best to see that Henry Miller paid—with his own life—one way or another. And he would like to join Mr. Richardson in personally getting his hands on him!

Feeling the hot emotion burning him with anger and hate—the same emotion he saw on Mr. Richardson's face—he felt an awful tug at his heart. He didn't want to hate. He didn't want to hurt. He didn't want to be the kind of person who was responsible for keeping another man behind bars, locked up for years, or even a lifetime. Is that what the Lord would want? Is that what Natalie would want? Revenge, hatred, bitterness, striking back—is that what he had taught his little girl?

With the image of his lovely, sweet daughter in his mind's eye, Jim could see her wearing that little white dove pin, the symbol of God's Spirit. *Is it God's Spirit in me at this moment? Can I practice what I have preached to my family?*

Jim took hold of the bottom of the bed to keep his knees from buckling. "Could we pray about this?"

"Pray?" Mrs. Richardson whispered as she slowly lifted her tearstained face from her hands. She said it as if it were a foreign word that she'd heard somewhere but didn't know the meaning. Then comprehension dawned, as if the word held hope. She nodded.

The scowl didn't leave Mr. Richardson's face, but he lowered his head and stared at the floor.

Jim took that as assent. Suddenly, the adrenaline that had kept him going seemed to melt, and he felt he could no longer stand on his feet. He fell to his knees beside the bed, braced his hands against the edge, closed his eyes, and prayed.

"Lord, forgive my bitter spirit. Put your loving spirit in our hearts that we might not hate and harm like those who do not have Jesus in their lives. We don't need any more evil in this world, Lord. We need you to give us courage to face whatever comes, strength to stand strong in times of adversity, hope that we will again find joy and beauty in the life you have given us. Thank you, God, for so richly blessing us with daughters that we love and the joy they have given us. You know where they are, Lord. You love them more than we do. If it be your will, return them to us. If it is not your will, help us to remember the good they brought to us and not dwell on the bad. Lord, we pray for this man in this bed. We thank you that his life was spared. Restore his health, Lord. And we pray for . . ."

Jim had to stop, stumbling over his sobbing words. He cleared his throat. "We pray for Henry Miller. I know these are the right words to say, Lord," he confessed. "Now help us to feel them. Let them become part of our thoughts and actions. Give us strength to live your way. Help us to remember that there are laws to punish criminals and that you are the final Judge of mankind. Forgive us our sins as we forgive those who sin against us. In Jesus' name. Amen."

Carl and the Richardsons said, "Amen," and so did Frank, who had drifted back into consciousness.

Jim got to his feet and reached for a tissue from the bedside table to wipe his tear-drenched face. He couldn't yet feel the words he knew were right. He hoped God would help him feel them, and help the Richardsons feel them, before either had the chance to get their hands on Henry Miller.

But . . . suppose Henry perished in that flood. Then, likely, he did not have a heavenly home with the Lord. At that instant, Jim Ainsworth could feel sorry for him. Even as his heart was heavy for his daughter, who already, whether she was in this world or her eternal home, had eternal life with God the Father.

A light knock sounded on the doorway.

A nurse stepped inside. After confirming the Richardsons' identity, she asked, "Valerie Miller is your daughter?"

"Yes, yes," they said quickly.

"She's being taken to the maternity ward," the

nurse said. "As soon as she's settled, you may go in to see her."

Mr. Richardson stared while Mrs. Richardson questioned. "Maternity ward . . . but she's not . . . is she?"

"I'm sorry, I don't know any details," the nurse said. "But we're overcrowded and are putting patients wherever we can find space."

"What about my daughter?" Jim asked. "Natalie Ainsworth?"

The nurse shook her head. "I don't know, sir."

Mr. Richardson took hold of Jim's arm. "Maybe Val can tell us something."

"I'm going, too," Frank said, now appearing wide awake and determined.

"No!" the nurse said. "You can't do that."

"I'm going," he insisted. "If I have to hobble on one foot, crawl, or fight every doctor and nurse in the hospital."

The nurse hurried away. Frank's parents tried to keep him in bed, but Frank wouldn't hear of it.

Soon, the nurse returned with a wheelchair for Frank to ride in.

Jim took a deep breath as they all prepared to visit with Valerie Miller. He was glad the Richardsons' daughter had been found. She was here.

Now where is my daughter? My precious Natalie?

Jim hung back when the Richardsons went into Valerie's room. Carl touched his arm in a consoling gesture and whispered that he would go make some phone calls. Frank was wheeled up to one side of the bed and the Richardsons walked to the other, surrounding the pale young woman Jim had seen in the emergency room.

With mixed emotions, Jim watched as Mr. Richardson's hands explored his daughter's face, like a blind person might do to determine how a person looked. Perhaps Mr. Richardson had to prove to himself that his daughter was really here—alive and well.

Then Mrs. Richardson bent over the girl, hugging her, crying, expressing her relief, asking questions that tumbled one over the other.

Frank took her hand and expressed his joy that she was safe. "Has Henry been found?" she asked.

"We don't know," Frank said.

The tears brimming in Val's eyes spilled over and ran down her cheeks.

Jim thought he'd waited long enough for the family reunion. He had to ask about Natalie. Just then, Val looked at him, startled. Before he could speak, she gasped, "You—you're looking for Henry!"

A moment passed before Jim realized what she meant. He was still wearing his prison uniform. He had likely been on duty a couple of times when Henry Miller's wife had visited. He didn't recognize her, but she certainly would have looked different from this obviously exhausted young woman with no makeup, matted hair, and a hospital gown.

"I'm not concerned about Henry right now," Jim said. "Do you know anything about Natalie? My daughter?" Jim asked.

"Natalie?" Val croaked. "Oh, this is worse than I thought." She covered her face with her hands.

"Please," Jim said.

Val nodded. Her mother pulled up a chair and sat near her daughter. Mr. Richardson stood behind his wife, holding on to the back of a chair. Val poured out the story—all she knew about Natalie. "I wondered at times," Val said, "if Natalie was an angel who had come to tell me that God loves me and that He could fix all the things that had gone wrong in my life."

Jim was shaking his head. "That's just Natalie's way."

Val nodded. "She was going to give me a pin that she wanted me to think about. A dove, she said, to remind me of God's Spirit. But she fell into the water . . . and disappeared. I closed my eyes then and just hung on to the tree limb, pretending that dove was with me. I don't know how much time passed before I heard a sound, like a huge dove, flapping its wings, and then someone was tying a rope around me, telling me everything was going to be all right and they wanted to get me into the helicopter. I blacked out then. I don't remember being rescued. I woke up in the emergency room."

The nurse, who had been waiting at the doorway, stepped closer. "She really needs her rest. The doctor said this would be good for her emotionally. But physically she's had a rough time. She hasn't eaten."

Val looked at her. "I can't. Not until I tell my family everything." Her words stopped, and again she covered her face with her hands.

"I'll leave," Jim offered.

"No," Val said, reaching toward him. "I mean, if you have to go, I understand. But you, being an officer, need to hear about Henry and me. Unless. . . ?"

Jim knew she meant unless he had to look for Natalie. But it was now in God's hands. He would continue to look, to search, to question, until he found answers. But he felt he did need to know whatever this young woman could say about Henry, herself, and Natalie.

Val sighed, seeming reluctant to say out loud what was on her mind. "I'm pregnant," she said after a moment. "That's why I'm still here. They've done some blood work and want to make sure the baby is all right before releasing me."

132

"A baby?" her mother said. "Oh, Val. How wonderful!" She looked up at her husband with a trembly smile. "Our first grandchild."

"I was going to have an abortion . . . today," Val admitted.

"Val, why?" her mother said, dumbfounded. "We don't believe in abortion. You never have."

"She hasn't been thinking straight," Mr. Richardson said. "With all the trouble Henry has put her through."

"The baby belongs to Henry, too," Val said.

"It's yours, Val," her mother said. "We love you, and we will love your child. You must move in with us and let us take care of you."

"I know I was wrong, Mama," Val admitted. She looked at Jim. "Natalie made me see that. I think I would have just welcomed that flood to take me away if it hadn't been for her. She talked about God as if He's . . . really real . . . and really cares . . . about me."

"Honey," her mother whispered, placing her hand on Val's shoulder.

"I want you to know that instead of giving my life to that sea of water last night, I gave it to God. I'm going to have my baby. That's why Henry escaped from prison. To talk some sense into me. He couldn't . . . but Natalie did."

She sobbed openly then. "I wouldn't have listened to anyone. I think . . . I think God let that flood happen, and let that girl be there with me, because I wouldn't listen to anyone otherwise. I was so scared, I listened. And after Natalie was gone, there was only me and God. I know He wants a better life for me, but I've done so much damage. I've lost Henry. I was going to get rid of our baby. I don't deserve to live."

"Yes, you do!" Jim said forcefully. "You deserve to live. Natalie told you what is right. God loves you and will give you a good life. He's spared your life for a reason. I know it looks hopeless right now. But it's not. With God, all things are possible."

"She said things like that," Val said, her face streaked with tears.

"If you need a home, you can stay with us," Jim said.

Val nodded, and her choked words were hardly audible. "That's what . . . Natalie said."

"You're our daughter, Val. You have a home with us if you want it," Mr. Richardson said.

Val shook her head. "Not after you hear what I have to say . . . you won't want me." She choked on a sob, then cleared her throat. "What Henry did—the embezzling—he did for me. It wasn't Henry who lost our money through gambling. It was me. He wouldn't tell on me. I begged him not to tell you. He did what he did because . . . he loved me and wanted to help me. But even last night, I rejected what he had to say. I'm the one who has a gambling habit. I tried to stop. I've been doing it for years. When you thought I was so conscientious for working summers and holidays, it wasn't that at all. It was to support my gambling habit. I did it all the time."

"I can't believe this," Mr. Richardson said. "Are you trying to protect Henry? Val, he embezzled from my bank. *He* did it."

"But he did it for me. Because he loved me."

"Hold it a minute!" Frank said. "Before anybody starts placing blame and making accusations, I need to confess my part in this."

His parents looked at him in astonishment.

"Haven't we heard enough?" Mr. Richardson said.

But Frank insisted. "I introduced Val to gambling. Remember how I took her out on her sixteenth birthday? Well, I never told you the truth about where we went. I took her to the Riverboat. I even provided her with a fake ID. I thought it would just be fun—a thrill. I didn't realize it was going to have such an effect on her. I should have. I know there are people who spend their last cent on gambling. I guess I never thought a sensible person like Val would do that. Henry talked to me about it last night. We were stuck together in that water for hours before we were rescued. He kept me alive by being there—stayed by my side and kept me talking so I wouldn't drift off and drown. And he talked all about Val. Said we all had to help her. I couldn't say much, but I heard him talking. He made me realize that, in a way, I'm more to blame than he is. I started all this. I'm to blame for Val's problem, and now for whatever has happened to Henry."

They all began to talk at once, trying to deny that others were to blame, apologizing, explaining.

Jim walked up and held on to the end of the bed. "It sounds like a lot of mistakes have been made here. Maybe it's just time to forgive, learn from the mistakes, and start over."

"You're right," Mr. Richardson said. "And the first thing we should do is help you find your daughter." He bent his head. "I haven't prayed aloud in a long time. But I'd like to now."

They all bowed their heads. Mr. Richardson stumbled through the prayer, tripping over some words, but he thanked God for bringing Frank and Val through the flood. He asked God to please keep their unborn grandchild healthy and to bring Val safely through her pregnancy. Then he thanked God for Natalie, whom he credited with having made a change in his family for the better. He asked God to be with the Ainsworths in a special way, as he had been with Val during the long, cold night. Then he lifted his head.

"Mr. Ainsworth," he said, "I don't know what to

ask for concerning your daughter. I don't know if I'm the one who should . . ."

"I don't know, either," Jim replied. "I know that Natalie is ready to meet her maker. I know that heaven is a better place to be than this earth. But I want my daughter home and safe. God knows what is best. I don't. Let's just pray that He will work in this situation, and that His will be done, even if it's not our will."

"Yes," Mr. Richardson said, and they all knew that Jim's words were his prayer.

Just then Carl returned from making his phone calls. "Jim," he said, "there's a patient in ER who just might be Henry Miller."

Fifteen

Henry was unable to open his eyes or speak a word, but he felt sure he now lay on something solid. He could hear his own shallow breathing. Taking in a full breath was painful. He tried to lift his arms, but they were confined. Handcuffs? Was he alive and cuffed to something?

"Wake up, Henry. We've got to talk to you." Fred Richardson's voice was penetrating his consciousness, like a nightmare.

"Who . . . what?" he mumbled.

"You're in the hospital," the voice said. "But we need to talk to you."

Hospital?

"I know you're hurting, man," said a voice that sounded like Frank, "but you've got to talk to us."

Yes, it was Frank's voice. But what about Val . . . and Natalie? Henry felt such mental anguish then, he wished to drift off into that never-never land again. He tried. The harder he tried, the more awake he became—and the more scared.

"My father's here, Henry," Frank said.

Henry lay waiting for the attack—verbal and perhaps physical, too. He couldn't blame them. Regardless of his intentions and his ignorance over the depth of Val's gambling addiction, he'd done wrong. He'd embezzled. He'd escaped. He'd stolen a car. He'd kid-napped a girl. He deserved whatever punishment came his way. Why couldn't he have just drowned?

Henry lay with hot tears scalding his eyes beneath his closed lids. Frank had not said Val was there. Like Frank, she wasn't a strong swimmer. Had that apple tree been too old and rotten to hold her? Had her branch broken, like Frank's had? Maybe he should have stayed with her—with his wife . . . and his child.

The physical pain didn't matter. He'd forever feel the emotional pain. He'd lost his wife. He'd lost his child.

And he couldn't tell Val's parents about her. He couldn't lie there and condemn her. He'd rather her parents keep the memory of her as the wonderful girl she was. Now there was no need to tell about the un-born baby. They didn't need to know about her gam-bling addiction.

"Henry!" It was Frank's voice again. "Mr. Ains-worth needs to ask you some questions. You have to wake up."

Mr. Ainsworth? Who? Why? Wait—isn't that an of-ficer at the prison? They've come for me!

"Natalie," he heard, and thought that must be the voice of Mr. Ainsworth. "You took her when you took the car at the college?"

"Yes," Henry said faintly.

"What happened to her?" he heard.

"In a tree, the last time I saw her. Don't know . . . anything else."

"Why did you do it, Miller?" The voice sounded so desperate. "Why did you take my daughter into that flood?"

Henry's eyes flew open then. He sucked in a deep breath, and the feeling was like an arrow straight through his heart. His own breath was stabbing him, but he didn't care. He wished it would kill him.

"Your . . . dau. . . ?" He could not say the words. It hurt too much. It was bad enough that he'd taken the girl. But now, it was more personal. He knew this man. Jim Ainsworth was the most respected officer at the prison—a fine Christian man. A good family man. He demanded that inmates respect the law, but he was fair. If a prisoner had a real problem, he could go to him, and Ainsworth would see that he had a chance to air his grievance. *Why didn't I go to Jim Ainsworth—instead of kidnapping his daughter?*

"No," Henry moaned. He was not seeing a prison officer's uniform now. He was seeing Jim Ainsworth's tear-drenched face that had aged ten years. He saw bloodshot eyes filled with pain. A man's concern for his child. *I was concerned about my unborn child—but not about Natalie—somebody else's child.* His every breath became a groan. "Die. I want to die."

"God spared your life for a reason, Henry," Jim said. "Maybe to give you another chance."

Henry couldn't believe what he was hearing. How could this man not attack him? He managed to gasp out the words, "You don't . . . hate me?"

"I'm trying not to, Henry," Jim said honestly. "It wouldn't change the situation. It would only change me into the kind of person I don't want to be. I need to spend my time trying to find my daughter and praying that God will give us all the strength to face whatever we must face."

"I'm sorry," Henry said, hardly able to get his breath. "But I can't expect . . ." He shook his head and turned his face away.

"Forgiveness?" Jim asked, his own voice a sob.

Henry couldn't answer.

"Henry," Jim said, determined, "the lives of my family are in the hands of One much greater than you.

But you've played a part in this. If Natalie is found alive and well, I will find it easy to forgive you. If she isn't, then I will pray—fervently—until I forgive you. God commands that. I don't think it will be easy. But with Him, it's possible." He paused, then his words were said above the tears in his voice. "God does a much better job with forgiveness than I do. It's available to you. He spared your life, Henry. The least you can do is live it—for Him."

With that, Jim turned and left the room. The pain Henry felt was overwhelming. Yet he welcomed it. He wanted to be punished.

Oh, God, God, forgive me, forgive me, Henry prayed within himself as he heard Jim Ainsworth telling someone, "I have to call home."

Henry wanted to ask about Val. But she and Natalie had both been together. Whatever happened to one probably happened to the other. He wished for someone to strike out at him, but even Mr. Richardson only said, "Come on, Frank. Henry's in no condition for us to talk to him."

Henry didn't think anyone would have told a nurse he was in pain. He hadn't even attempted to push the button and ask for medicine, feeling he deserved any pain that came his way. But a nurse walked in and had him put a pill in his mouth and wash it down with water. It must have been pain medication, for he drifted off into a troubled sleep, trying, but unable, to forget the people he'd loved, the people he'd harmed. And he was asking God for forgiveness but didn't see how that could help this situation.

A long time later, Henry felt himself again being lifted out of the flood nightmare, and he sensed a presence in the room. He didn't want to look, didn't want to face whoever or whatever was there.

"Henry," he heard. A whispered voice said his name, and a hand, small and warm, slipped into his. "I love you, Henry. Can you ever forgive me? You have to wake up and hear this."

Love? Forgiveness?

In spite of himself, his eyes flew open. Next to him on a chair sat Val, pale but smiling at him, her eyes brimming with tears. She hadn't looked at him with such genuine affection in a long time . . . so long.

"Val? You're okay?" he rasped.

"Yeah," she said, "except I had to sneak down here. I'm wearing mom's coat over the dress of the day." She held open the coat to reveal a hospital gown.

"Matches the ones they brought in for me," he said.

"There's a guard outside, but Mr. Ainsworth asked him to let me come in. They know you're not terrible, Henry."

"The baby, Val?" he asked.

"She's fine," she said.

"She?" he questioned. "You know it's a girl?"

"It's too soon to tell, but I feel sure our baby is a girl." She sniffed. "From all indications, everything's fine. The hospital wants me to stay overnight for observation so they can be sure the baby's okay. And, Henry," she said, "I told the truth to Mom, Dad, Frank, and Mr. Ainsworth. They all know everything. All the awful things I've done and planned to do. Mom and Dad forgave me, Henry, and they aren't angry with you anymore. I'm going back home to live. Dad said most of what you did was making foolish mistakes and not from a desire to hurt anyone. He and Mom and Frank will all speak up for you if there's a trial."

"There will be," Henry said. "I knew when I planned to escape from prison that I'd be caught and they'd add years to my sentence. And I knew if I found a car, I'd be charged with car theft." He drew in a breath and grimaced, raising his hand to his bound chest.

"I'll wait for you, Henry," Val promised. "No matter how long it takes."

Henry was openly crying now. "I can't ask you to wait, Val. If Natalie isn't found . . . alive . . . then I'll never get out of prison. If she's not found, I'll be facing a life sentence." He inhaled deeply and lay back with his eyes squeezed shut. "Or worse. I'll have . . . death . . . facing me."

After a long moment, he heard her voice again. "Henry, we all faced death out there in the flood. Natalie told me to ask God for help. I did. I've given my life to Him, Henry. He saved me and you and Frank by having Natalie with us. And He saved our souls, Henry. No matter what happens to us now, we already have eternal life."

Henry was nodding. "I learned all those things many years ago, Val. But I turned from them. I'm not sure that God will forgive me for that." Henry looked toward the place where his unborn child was growing. "But He has saved the life of our child."

Val was crying and nodding. "Out there in that tree, alone, in the dark, with nothing to cling to but the hope Natalie had given me with her words about God, I promised Him, if He saved the baby, I would name her Natalie."

Sixteen

Rescue boats were out . . . rescue vehicles . . . ambulances . . . helicopters . . . and people of all kinds were more than willing to go into the flooded areas to help those in need.

TV and radio were reporting that many had lost their lives, their possessions, their homes, their loved ones. Neighbors and complete strangers went to help. They sent food to the workers. They sent cards of condolence and good will. They sent their prayers.

The churches in Garden City were packed with people who knew Natalie, and others who had heard about her over TV and by word of mouth.

Jill Ainsworth stayed home to be near the phone. The public now knew what Jim had told her earlier. Natalie had been kidnapped by Henry Miller. The prisoner had been rescued and was in Mercy Hospital with broken ribs. Natalie had sought safety in a tree with Valerie Miller but had fallen into the floodwaters and was swept away. An area search was under way. News and camera crews were now gathered on the front lawn of the Ainsworth home, awaiting any further details and trying to interview anyone who came in or out of the house.

Others were missing, too. The water had risen more quickly and higher than had been expected. The floodgates at the levee had been opened to prevent worse damage and destruction. Already it was declared a disaster area by the president of the United States. It could have been worse, they said, had they not opened the floodgates.

Jill believed that. Lives and property had certainly been saved by that action. Jim had even said Natalie was responsible for saving the life of Valerie Miller—the wife of the man who caused Natalie to be in that harrowing situation.

Jill understood all that. She was glad more lives hadn't been lost—or more homes ruined and more property damaged. Mr. and Mrs. Richardson had called from Mercy Hospital, expressing their deep regret and concern over Natalie, but also praising her for what she had done for their own daughter—saving her life, and the life of her unborn child, and bringing her to the Lord. By so doing, Natalie had renewed their own faith in God and had given them hope for the future. Jill was glad for that—it was typical of Natalie.

A message from Valerie Miller said she was praying for Natalie. The hospital had allowed her to fax a letter to the police, who then brought it to Jill. It was a long letter, praising Natalie. Henry had written a note at the end of it. *I'm sorry for what I did to your daughter*, he wrote. *But I want you to know what she did for me. For so long, I saw only my failures, my sins, and God's wrath. When I was with Natalie and listened to her talk, I saw God's love. She made me believe that maybe God will still forgive me. I wish she were safe and I were the one missing.*

All of that was wonderful, even consoling, but it did not lessen Jill's deep concern and fear about Natalie's whereabouts. If the worst happened, she had no doubt that Natalie would be with her heavenly Father forever, in a wonderful place, never to have any sorrow or fear anymore. Never any sickness or pain. Never have her heart bleed, as Jill's was doing at this moment. She would never have such heartache, such heaviness.

And such joy. . . ! Jill thought. *Natalie has been a bright spot—so good—such a wonderful gift to us all. But I miss her so. I know God only loaned her to me, but I'd like to have her . . . a little longer. But your will be done,* she prayed with her mind. *Return her to me,* she prayed with her heart.

Jill tried to be brave for her three other daughters. Each was so special in her own way. She wanted to keep her darling, precious children close to her forever, much like a mother hen who covers her chicks with her wings.

Wings! Jill looked out the kitchen window and saw a break in the clouds. There was a patch of blue up there, a reminder that every cloud has a silver lining. There is a heaven beyond this earth. *Oh, thank you, God, that my Natalie has a home with you forever. Thank you, God, that, although I can't begin to fathom it, you love my daughter more than I do. Don't let her be suffering, Lord, please. Take care of our Natalie.*

She couldn't break down in front of the children. And she was grateful that their closest friends were there. Maureen Ryan had stayed with Jill throughout the long night. Her seven-year-old son, Justin, had declared staunchly, his brown eyes flashing and his rust-colored hair bouncing in curls, "I'll be the man of the house here. I'll stay right by Rose until we hear something."

Justin had accepted Jesus as his personal Savior and Lord at Christmastime. His sister, Ruthie, had always called him "monster," but now he was reminding them all of what they should be thinking. Just stay calm . . . until they heard something.

In the living room, Natalie's sisters, Amy, Sarah, and Rose, were talking with their friends, praying, and listening to the latest report on flood victims and damage . . . and the search for Natalie.

———

It was Friday afternoon when Sean Jacson walked into the fellowship hall at Garden City Community Church, where the youth group was meeting to pray for Natalie and the many victims of the worst flood to hit the area in over fifty years.

There'd been a TV report that the prisoner had admitted kidnapping Natalie. They weren't going to make a celebrity of him by putting him on TV, but his wife was going to make a statement at three o'clock.

Looking around the fellowship hall, Sean remembered that these people used to be his friends, and he wanted them to know that he cared what happened to Natalie—that he wasn't completely heartless. He sat down in a chair at the back of the room, already darkened so everybody could focus on the TV up front. The room was packed. A couple of people looked at him in the dim light and nodded, as if to welcome him. Andy Kelly, the youth director, walked by and placed his hands on Sean's shoulders for a second and handed him a Styrofoam cup of hot chocolate.

The reporter was announcing the upcoming interview from Mercy Hospital and said that Natalie Ainsworth still hadn't been found. At three, the camera scanned a room that looked like an office, then focused in on a middle-aged couple, introduced as Fred Richardson, president of a bank in Cape Girardeau, his wife, Virginia, their son, Frank, who had a cast on his arm and another on his foot, and their daughter, Valerie Richardson Miller, sitting in a wheelchair.

The reporter explained that Valerie Miller had a statement to make, then the camera focused on her.

"We're not excusing Henry at all," Valerie began.

"He isn't excusing himself. But I want the viewing audience to know how sorry we are that Natalie Ainsworth got caught up in this family situation of ours. Henry was wrong; he knows that. But I want you to know what that young girl did for us. Henry and I were at the point of not caring anymore about our lives. We'd really messed up. But Natalie made us believe that God loves us and cares about us. She made me see there is hope for the future. She pointed us to God, and to His Son, Jesus Christ.

"I'm not saying this as any kind of excuse, but to tell you out there that what seems like your own business, your own money, your own life, is not that at all. If you don't have the power of God in your lives, then you have power from a different source. Things like gambling can become an obsession. It ruined our lives. But it can only destroy us if we let it, if we bring it into our lives. Then it can become a disease that we have no power to stop.

"Our hearts go out to the friends and family of Natalie Ainsworth. We are praying for her, and we ask for the prayers of all who hear this. Because of my sins, that girl is missing. Because of her faith, my family has a new life, a new beginning."

The other Richardsons stated much of the same, praising Natalie, blaming themselves, reaching out to the hearers.

Sean stopped listening to the TV and thought hard about what Valerie Miller had just said. Could gambling really become a disease and ruin your life? He'd never really thought much about it. It had seemed like harmless fun. He looked around the room. He knew most of the kids here. The names of most of the guys, and a lot of the girls, had been on his betting charts more than once. Was this more than an innocent game?

What about Ruthie? Deep down, he knew she

didn't approve of gambling. Maybe she had good reason after all. If he was ever going to win Ruthie's heart again, it wouldn't be with betting.

Sean had thought he was doing so well—turning away from the drug scene, getting along better with his dad. He had really thought he was a better person now, but the whole tragedy with Natalie—and now hearing Valerie's testimony—brought it all into focus for the first time. He'd listened to preachers go on about sin and had inwardly scoffed at all that, but now it hit him: He was wrong. What he was doing now—how he was living now—was no better than what he was before. And he had no power to change it. What was it Andy was always telling them? *"The only way to turn bad situations into good is to give them over to the Lord."*

Sean suddenly knew what he had to do. He got up and walked over to Andy, who was standing in the doorway of the kitchen.

"Can I talk to you?" Sean asked. "It's really important."

"Sure," Andy said, putting his arm around Sean's shoulders and leading him to a chair in the kitchen.

Ruthie had been sitting near the back of the hall and had seen Sean come in earlier but refused to look at him. After the interview on TV, Stephanie Kelly, Andy's wife and co-youth director, said, "If anybody could get through an ordeal like this and bring good from it, it would be Natalie."

They all agreed, and Stephanie led them in prayer.

Ruthie knew Stephanie was right. How many people would not totally panic if kidnapped by a prisoner? Only Natalie would try to convert him!

After the "amen," the group began milling around, getting something to eat and drink, expressing their disbelief that this could have happened to Natalie, and glancing toward the TV for any special reports.

Then, to her surprise, she saw Sean sitting in the kitchen talking to Andy. For an instant those old feelings returned. She remembered that she had loved Sean not too long ago. What she had thought could never change *had* changed.

Could that be true for Natalie, too? She turned away from the group she'd been standing with and began to cry. Then she felt a hand touch hers in a comforting gesture.

Sean?

She looked. No, it was Stick Gordon. Her feelings for him had changed, too. Until a few months ago, she'd thought of Stick as the class clown. Not anymore. When she'd had so much trouble with Sean, Stick had turned out to be a friend with a heart of gold.

The look in Stick's eyes seemed to say he knew how she felt. She thought he did. His grandpa had cerebral palsy and was slowly dying. Stick had to face that daily.

Looking into his eyes, she knew he was thinking the same thing that was in her mind.

Natalie might be dead.

But they wanted her alive.

Heaven was better than earth, yes. They all knew that. But it was just too hard to face. First, Natalie should have graduation . . . college . . . marriage . . . children . . . a career . . . and . . . Scott.

"How is she?" Scott asked the minute he ran up to Cissy, who had come to pick him up at the small airport in Garden City. The storm had finally broken up and moved east, allowing the airport to reopen. Scott had flown in on the Carlos' private jet.

As soon as he'd entered the terminal, he spied Cissy's tall, sleek figure topped by her corn-silk blond hair.

"They haven't found her yet, Scott," she said, her blue eyes tired and scared. "They found all the people she was with, but they haven't found her. The whole town is praying. It's on the news. In the morning papers. Dad is in touch with every hospital, giving priority to any news about Natalie. They caught the prisoner. Apparently, Natalie converted them all before—"

"Before?" Scott blurted.

"We don't know, Scott."

He raked his fingers through his hair. As they raced toward Cissy's car, all he could think about were the things he should have done . . . or not done. "I should never have taken that modeling job. I should have stayed here, finished high school with her. I'm going to give up modeling, Cissy. She's done so much for me. How could I have put my career ahead of her?"

"Oh, Scott. I know how you feel. If I hadn't invited her to my house, to show off and tell her all about *my* life, she wouldn't have been out in the storm in the first place. This would never have happened. It's all my fault."

Scott was silent as they got into the car and Cissy pulled out onto the highway, heading into town. After a long moment, he said, "It seemed so right, what I was doing. It was going to help me get a job as a photographer. I was doing it for *us*—so that someday Natalie and I could be together always."

"I know," Cissy said. "And she helped me so much. Made me see that God in my life was so much more important than modeling or acting. And yet I felt God had opened the door to these jobs. I thought Natalie would be so pleased that I was involved with Christian modeling now."

"She would be," Scott said. "Who'd have imagined she'd be kidnapped and . . . and . . ."

His voice trailed off. He didn't want to think the worst. Only a few months ago, she'd gone to New York with him, his mom, Cissy, and her mom. They'd all returned to Garden City, but he'd stayed in New York to get on with his photography and modeling career. He remembered Natalie saying, "I'll see you at graduation."

"And don't forget our promise to each other, Nat," Scott had said softly.

Would they be able to keep that promise now?

Suddenly, he felt very, very cold.

Seventeen

The helicopters couldn't fly much longer. It would soon be dark. All the areas where Natalie might be had been thoroughly searched, not only by air, but also by boat and on foot.

Jim Ainsworth wasn't allowed on the rescue vehicles, but a friend of Dr. Stiles offered his own private helicopter. Jim and Carl were in the copter with the pilot and a medical assistant.

A rainbow had been sighted earlier. That meant hope. So did all the prayers being offered up in Natalie's behalf.

From high above the treetops, Jim could see rescue boats down around the farmhouse. The house had been searched again, but no one was there. The water was calm now, and boats could prowl the area. Animals and debris were washed up on the banks several miles above Tanis.

"I'll take us farther downstream," the pilot said, but that was out of range of where victims were expected.

The pilot followed the ribbon of water that ran through towns, across fields, over highways. They were moving away from the areas where most of the damage had been done.

"On your left," shouted the medical attendant.

Jim immediately turned his head and stared through

the binoculars. He saw what the attendant had seen. A lifeless figure washed up on the bank. No one spoke for a long moment. It was a female, lying on her back. Long light brown hair streamed out from her head. She was wearing jeans and a cream-colored jacket. How could she have been carried so far downstream?

"That's her," Jim choked out with what little air he had, for the sight took his breath. "That's my Natalie."

No one shouted for joy. No one spoke further. The chopping of the rotor was a deafening roar. On the brown earth, amid debris, the figure lay motionless, with one arm bent at the elbow and the other lying across her chest.

The clouds parted and a golden ray of sun shone on the lifeless-looking figure. Something on her jacket, next to her hand, began to shine. Jim knew it was the pin Natalie boldly wore as an expression of her inner faith.

With tears streaming down his cheeks, a picture from the Scriptures penetrated Jim's mind. The Holy Spirit, like a dove, alighted on the shoulders of Jesus. The clouds opened, and the voice of God spoke, "This is my beloved son, in whom I am well pleased."

Jim felt the words echo in his mind as he focused on the shining symbol of God's Spirit. *This is my beloved daughter* resounded over and over as the helicopter rotor whirred and the sun shone. The little dove danced and sparkled, and they drew nearer, nearer. *This is my beloved daughter . . . in whom I have always been well pleased.*

———

The fact that Natalie's hair had been entangled in tree branches was what the rescuers felt had probably saved her life and allowed her to be washed up on a bank farther downstream than where the search crews had initially looked. Perhaps that kept her face out of the water, floating on her back, so that she hadn't drowned.

But no one knew for sure. Only that she'd had a hard blow on the head and was in a coma. When, or if, she might come out of it, the doctors couldn't say. They'd done all they could. It was out of their hands now. If she did regain consciousness, there could be brain damage.

People who had known Natalie, or had heard about her, were wearing white ribbons to say they were praying for her recovery.

Dr. Stiles arranged for the Ainsworth family to have a couple of rooms at the hospital. Scott went home at night, but he stayed there during the day, and he talked to Natalie's friends who came to find out about her but weren't allowed to see her.

The words they'd long awaited finally came.

It was the afternoon of the third day after she'd been brought in.

"She's talking and asking questions." Both Dr. Stiles and the administrator of Mercy Hospital had come down themselves to report the good news.

"Thank God," said Andy Kelly as he looked at the young people who had crowded around. Ruthie, Stick, Cissy, Scott, and several from the youth group wanted to hear every word the doctors had to say.

"Is she all right?" Jim asked anxiously.

It's what they all were thinking.

An ominous silence followed as the two administrators glanced at each other, worry furrowing their brows.

"Physically she will be fine," said Dr. Stiles, "but—"

"But what?" came the immediate question from Jim and Jill.

"She has not completely recovered her memory. That may take time."

"But she will?" asked Jim.

"We can't really say. She didn't know me, Jim. Try not to be too disappointed if she doesn't know any of you."

Only family were allowed into her room. But Scott was Dr. Stiles' nephew, and the administrator was his friend. The Ainsworths weren't about to exclude him.

"Come on, Scott," Mr. Ainsworth said as they hurried to Natalie's room.

Scott knew! The moment he looked into Natalie's eyes, he knew she didn't know him. His heart began to pound. Would she ever remember him?

She's alive! kept sounding in Scott's mind. *I am thankful for that. But I want her to know how much I care. Will I ever mean anything to her again?* He looked into her eyes, which held only a blank stare . . . and the pain of trying to recognize them. Scott kept remembering when he himself had been in the hospital, when his head was shaved, when none of that made any difference to Natalie. And it made no difference now that her head was bandaged, that her face was almost as pale as the white sheets.

But it did matter that she looked at them with no spark of recognition, only deep, dark forgetfulness in her eyes.

Yet all his memories were piling up inside him. He could never forget Natalie. How could she forget him?

When he was in New York and tempted to go out with some of the beautiful models, he'd look at the snow dome she'd given him and remember Natalie, the pretty girl with what he thought was the most beautiful spirit and the most wonderful personality in the world. Famous models had nothing on her.

He remembered holding Natalie in his arms while the snow fell around them. He'd savored the fragrance of her light brown hair when she laid her head against his chest, where his heart was pounding.

He remembered looking into her deep blue eyes and saying, "I love you, Natalie."

"I love you, too, Scott," she had said, and even now he could feel the warmth of their lips as they touched.

Never, never would he forget her. She was special. She'd given him more than her declaration of love. She'd made him realize how great was God's love and concern for him. She'd made all the difference in his life.

Natalie, he whispered within himself, *please don't leave me. Please don't forget me.*

Natalie lay on the bed with her head only slightly raised. She wanted to sit up, but the doctors had said she shouldn't just yet. She looked around at the crowd of visitors surrounding her bed. How full of love and concern they all seemed!

The woman touched her gently, asking tenderly, "Do you know us, darling?"

Natalie searched their faces and struggled to fight away the panic that rose inside her. "The nurse said that you're my family."

"Yes, I'm your mother," the woman said, and Natalie could tell she was choking back tears. "The doctors said for us not to tire you out with questions, darling. There will be plenty of time to talk later." She bent over and kissed Natalie on the forehead, then introduced the others by name.

The man came nearer. "Kitten, I can't tell you how good it is to see you lying here. We have so much to be thankful for."

Natalie felt like nodding, but the slightest move of her head made it feel heavy, and instinct told her to be still, as the doctors had instructed.

But she could smile.

And she did. At all of them. The three girls at the foot of the bed were all trying to tell her things at the same time, interrupting each other, apologizing, asking if they should be talking about certain things.

Natalie wasn't sure. She didn't know what all had happened, but she'd been told she was safe and well. She felt very tired and knew she'd been in a coma for a few days. The doctors said fatigue was normal.

She was on medication and figured that accounted for her blurry vision. But someone else was there. The tall figure, named Scott, did not have the family resemblance. And he was so good-looking, she could hardly take her eyes from him. "Are you . . . my brother?" she asked.

His eyes held a moment of shock, then pain, as he mumbled, "No, I'm . . . a friend," and turned his head to look out the window. Natalie followed his gaze and saw gray clouds hastening across the sky.

A special friend? she wondered. But she didn't know him. Everything seemed awkward suddenly. Her mom was now stroking her hand, and she noticed something. "You're all wearing white ribbons," she said.

"Everyone's wearing them," her mom said. "For you."

"I appreciate that," she said and in the awkward silence looked out the window. The gray clouds seemed to have turned white and were skittering across the sky, revealing patches of blue. A ray of sunshine broke through the clouds and streaked through the window, outlining Scott in an aura of gold.

Suddenly, like rushing water, memories flooded her head. She felt like storms were closing in on her, and with them was the fear she had felt in the cold waters. Breath was scarce as she relived her sense of panic. Then the sun glinted on something above the white ribbon on Amy's shirt.

Natalie felt as if her vision was clearing, just as the sky was doing. But then, suddenly, the tears came again as other memories surfaced. Memories of joy and happiness and peace.

"I know what that is," Natalie said, looking at the pin on Amy's shirt. And she remembered when she had pinned her own on the outside of her jacket, when she'd been so afraid of what Henry Miller might do to her. She remembered thinking then that Jesus had promised to be with her always. And He had been. And He was.

"The little white dove," she whispered, and looking around she saw the hope in her family's eyes.

"And I know you, Amy."

Her beautiful sister glowed almost as brightly as the sunshine, now streaming through the window. "Yes, I'm Amy."

"I mean, I really know. I know you, too, Sarah. And Rose. I remember . . . you all."

While her family began expressing delight that her memory was returning, she saw the movement at the window. Her handsome friend was turning. She felt a great lump in her throat, a great joy in her heart, and when their eyes met, she knew he would know.

"Scott," she whispered.

The sudden twitch of his lips and joy in his eyes told her that he knew she remembered. "Natalie," he said, and it was such a beautiful sound.

Her family made room for him as he walked near. He seemed to forget the family, and so did Natalie as he said, "It's so good to know you're going to be okay."

Unable to take her eyes from Scott's, she heard the voice of the nurse saying they'd have to leave. "Let's give them a moment," she heard her dad say.

The nurse held the door open while her family exited. Then her redheaded best friend, Ruthie, with tears streaming down her freckled face, stuck her head in the door and yelled, "I love you, Natalie." Flanking her was a tall, lanky boy making goofy faces and waving at her. Then he began making victory signs with his fingers. *Stick!* She remembered!

"Oh, you kids," the nurse said as she shooshed them away from the door. But not before Natalie saw Stick put his arm around Ruthie in a comforting manner. Ruthie leaned her head against his chest.

"Now *that*—I don't remember!" Natalie said. "Those two have always been at each other's throats."

"You know what they say about hate being closely related to love," Scott said.

Love, Natalie was thinking as the nurse closed the door, leaving her and Scott alone. She remembered very well the feeling of love.

Scott pulled up a chair and sat close to the bed and took her hand in his. "Don't ever forget me again," he pleaded.

Moisture welled up in Natalie's eyes. "Oh, Scott. Even when I couldn't remember, I was glad to hear that you were a friend and not a brother. I wanted to know you . . . better."

Scott's lips spread into his wonderful smile. "I think there's a saying about a friend sticking closer than a brother. I intend to do that."

Natalie's smile matched his. And as he bent his head toward hers, she didn't mind losing her memory. At the moment, all she wanted to remember was the touch of his hand on hers and the feel of his lips on hers . . . and the words that sounded like music, accompanied by each beat of her own heart—"I love you, Natalie."

Teen Series From
Bethany House Publishers

Early Teen Fiction (11–14)

THE ALLISON CHRONICLES by Melody Carlson
Follow along as Allison O'Brian, the daughter of a famous 1940s movie star, searches for the truth about her past and the love of a family.

HIGH HURDLES by Lauraine Snelling
Show jumper DJ Randall strives to defy the odds and achieve her dream of winning Olympic Gold.

SUMMERHILL SECRETS by Beverly Lewis
Fun-loving Merry Hanson encounters mystery and excitement in Pennsylvania's Amish country.

THE TIME NAVIGATORS by Gilbert Morris
Travel back in time with Danny and Dixie as they explore unforgettable moments in history.

Young Adult Fiction (12 and up)

CEDAR RIVER DAYDREAMS by Judy Baer
Experience the challenges and excitement of high school life with Lexi Leighton and her friends.

GOLDEN FILLY SERIES by Lauraine Snelling
Tricia Evanston races to become the first female jockey to win the sought-after Triple Crown.

JENNIE MCGRADY MYSTERIES by Patricia Rushford
A contemporary Nancy Drew, Jennie McGrady's sleuthing talents bring back readers again and again.

LIVE! FROM BRENTWOOD HIGH by Judy Baer
The staff of an action-packed teen-run news show explores the love, laughter, and tears of high school life.

THE SPECTRUM CHRONICLES by Thomas Locke
Adventure and romance await readers in this fantasy series set in another place and time.

SPRINGSONG BOOKS by various authors
Compelling love stories and contemporary themes promise to capture the hearts of readers.

WHITE DOVE ROMANCES by Yvonne Lehman
Romance, suspense, and fast-paced action for teens committed to finding pure love.

9711